Also by Stacey Wallace Benefiel

Glimmer (Zellie Wells Book Two)

Glow (Zellie Wells Book Three)

Day of Sacrifice Series

The Toilet Business (essays)

Glimpse

Stacey Wallace Benefiel

Published by Stacey Wallace Benefiel

ISBN: 1-4528-5874-8

www.staceywallacebenefiel.com

Second Edition

Cover design by Valerie Wallace

For Valerie and Sarah

Chapter One

I stared at the back of Avery Adams head, imagining what it would feel like to press my face into his wavy brown hair. I longed to experience the exhilaration of running my fingertips over his broad shoulders and down his chest, of standing that close to him, feeling the heat coming off of his golden skin.

He was two people ahead of me in the line to take communion. I tried to focus on the smell of his shampoo. Unfortunately, the two people between us were my mom, and his dad. With them blocking the way, all I could smell was tea rose perfume and extra strength drain cleaner. Not a pleasant combination.

The line moved forward. The woman behind me, Mrs. Hobby, stepped on the back of my heel, scraping it with the pointy toe of her white patent leather flat.

"Ouch!" I said, way too loudly. The congregants of my white bread Lutheran church were not prone to exclamation of any kind. I flushed my usual shade of flame as everyone looked at me, including Avery. Mortified, I wheeled around, facing Mrs. Hobby, accidentally knocking off her massive white Easter hat. I caught it mid-air and jammed it back on her head. "Sorry! I was spacing out," I whispered, like the whole church couldn't hear what I was saying.

"Zellie!" Mom hissed at me from the front of the church.

"Uh, here we go, our turn at bat." I ran up to the altar and knelt down, bowing my head, touching my chin to my chest.

Someone in the back of the church snorted a laugh. It sounded like Claire. A giggle shimmied up my throat.

Claire was my best friend and a frequent witness to my extreme dorkiness. She could also make me get the giggles at the most inappropriate moments.

I raised my head and took the communion wafer that my dad, Pastor Paul, offered, clamping my mouth shut before the giggles could escape and embarrass me even further. I glanced down the altar, wishing that the elder would hurry up with my tiny plastic cup of wine. I always seemed to get the communion wafer stuck to the roof of my mouth and then had to engage in some major tonguing in order to get it loose.

Avery leaned forward, taking his wafer from my dad. He swallowed it in one smooth gulp and then gave me a confused grin.

Oh, God, he must think I'm looking at him! I immediately stopped trying to pry the wafer loose with my tongue and put my chin to my chest again. What could I have looked like? I tried to float above myself, picture my face. What I conjured was not a flattering image. I had one eye closed, nostrils flaring, my tongue flicking back and forth. What the hell was my problem? I looked like a cat coughing up a fur ball. Ugh.

When everyone was served communion, I got up, avoiding my dad's bemused look and went back to the second pew where me, my mom and my sister Melody always sit.

Melody shook her head and flicked me on the back of my arm as I stepped past her and sat down in the pew. "Way to make a butt of yourself, Zel," she whispered into my ear.

"Whatever, hose beast." I flicked her on the knee and scooted away from her, closer to Mom.

She rolled her eyes at me. "Like I even know what that means."

Dad stepped up to the pulpit and shuffled his notes around in his hands. He was old school, writing his sermons in longhand on yellow legal pad paper. Assistant Pastor Morris wrote his on a computer and then downloaded it onto his BlackBerry, like someone from this century.

The sermon was my favorite part of the church service, not because my dad was such a charismatic speaker or anything, but because I could get in some good Avery daydreaming time. And, since he didn't know I was alive, daydream time was the only quality time I got to spend with him.

I leaned forward and put my forehead against the pew in front of me, rubbing my temples as though I had a headache. Turning my head the smallest increment to the side, I looked past my mom across the aisle to where Avery sat.

He was so beautiful it kinda hurt my heart to look at him. Ah well, I was in church after all, let the self flagellation commence!

I began at his feet. Polished black dress shoes, black socks slouching at the ankles, a glimpse of beautiful calf, his khaki pants hiked up just a little.

Moving up, I lingered on his hand resting atop his knee, his long, thin fingers spread out. I took a deep breath and envisioned reaching out my hand and intertwining my fingers with his. Running my thumb across the top of his hand from wrist to knuckle, brushing my fingertips up his forearm.

In my imagination I was sitting next to him, pressing the side of my thigh against his, then elbow to elbow, shoulder to shoulder. My lips grazed the bend of his neck, the line of his jaw, the corner of his mouth, across his lips. Then we were forehead to forehead, my hands in his hair, I inhaled him in--

"Ow!" I sat up straight, smarting from the sharp elbow to the ribs Melody had given me.

"It's time to sing!" She yanked me up and thrust an open hymnal into my hands.

On pastor's daughter autopilot, I sang, "Christ our Lord is risen today, haaaaaa-le-loo-oo-yah!"

"Hazel Grace Wells, you are going to burn a hole in the back of Avery's head as hard as you were staring at him." Mom turned from the driver's seat of our navy blue minivan, which was only six months younger than me. "Don't think I couldn't feel you looking, and in church of all places! How would you feel if your father had noticed you concentrating more on Avery than on God? He would not have appreciated it, young--"

"Mom, you're about to drive into Mrs. Woodbury's mailbox."

She whipped her head back around, swerving away from the Woodburys fiberglass mailbox.

"Dang it!" She pulled the minivan off of the gravel shoulder and back onto the black top.

"Gee, Mom," I said, a smirk spreading across my mouth, "what would Dad think of *you* concentrating on *me* concentrating on Avery while you're driving? I don't think he would appreciate it very much."

"Zip it, Zellie."

I caught Mom's eyes in the rearview mirror and locked on a reflection so much like my own it was freaky. We have the same long auburn hair and green eyes, the same hot pink flush across our cheeks.

Even though Mom grew up in Rosedell and everybody knows who we are, I was forever getting lame joke-y questions about my "older sister." Well, as much as we looked the same, Melody and Mom acted the same. It's not like I want to be Grace's (and she would kill me if I ever called her that in real life) clone or something.

Mom took the exit just past Wal-Mart off of Rosedell's main drag onto the highway. I watched the scenery go by at 55 miles an hour as we passed the lake and the lava rock fields getting closer to Mt. Scott and to the edge of town. She parked the minivan in front of the See-Saw diner, our usual Sunday lunch place.

We slid into opposite sides of a red vinyl booth. The waitress, Jan, was right behind us, plopping water glasses down on the yellow Formica table.

"Happy Easter ladies!" she said. "Two burgers, two chocolate shakes for here, two BLT's to-go?" She was already writing it down on her order pad.

"Just for me and Zel today, Jan," Mom said. "Paul and Melody are going to have Easter lunch at the Wallaces."

She crossed out part of the order. "Okay, I'll get this in for you and be back with the shakes in a jiff."

Mom dug around in her enormous brown leather purse until she found a small notebook. She flipped through the pages, stopping about halfway. "Ready for today's roster?"

This was a guessing game the two of us played every Sunday before we visited ill members of the congregation. I was pretty good at it and getting better the older I got, but Mom was exceptional. I nodded my head. "Ready."

"Jerry Hill. On previous occasions we have visited him for gout, appendicitis, and tennis elbow."

I closed my eyes and saw Mr. Hill sitting in his cushy beige recliner in the family room of his ranch house, watching the farm report on his dinky TV. He had a blanket tucked up under his chin. His eyes and nose were red. "Pfft! Easy," I said, giving Mom a "really?" look, "He's just got a cold, maybe a touch of hay fever. Next."

"Let's see if I can find a harder one," she scanned the page. "All right, here we go. Lanie Graham. We haven't visited her before and she only attends church once a month."

I chewed on my bottom lip, trying to concentrate. This one was way difficult. I couldn't picture what she looked like at all. "This is a hard one. Let me think...I feel like it has something to do with her eyes..." An image popped into my head of an older lady with cloudy eyes. I could hear the sound of a monitor beeping. Two words floated into my consciousness. "Cataract surgery?" I guessed. Mom looked both a little bit proud and a little bit worried, if that was possible. I slapped the table with my hand. I knew I was right.

Jan brought our order. "Right again, huh?" She smiled at me, shaking her head back and forth. "I do not know how you do that."

I shrugged my shoulders. I wasn't entirely sure how I did it either, I just did. "It runs in the family, Mom's really good at it too. I won't even let her guess anymore, she never misses."

Mom stuck the notebook back into her purse and waved my comment away. "Ah, it's a stupid parlor trick. You just have to trust your gut."

I sat at Mr. Hill's kitchen table staring up at the feed store calendar on the fridge. It featured a herd of cattle in a dusty pasture flanked by grey-blue mountains. The slogan "Rosedell Beef-*Central to Oregon*" was emblazoned across the expansive blue sky. When I looked out the window above the sink, I saw pretty much the same scene with the addition of a ranch hand burning trash in the far corner of the field. *De-pressing*. I drummed my fingers on the table to up my excitement level.

After about a minute of that, I got up and went to the black rotary phone on the wall. Lots of people in Rosedell still had old-timey phones. Again, *de-pressing*. I picked up the receiver and held the phone to my ear. I listened for a dial tone. It hummed back at me.

It was sort of against the rules for me to use other people's phones without asking. I knew that, but if I were a regular teenager and not like, what my parents expected me to be, a future bride of Jesus or whatever, I would be allowed to have a cell phone. Then, when I was having a weirdly bitchy off day I could go out to the minivan and talk to Claire about my upcoming birthday party or Avery or lava rock formation, instead of stewing in my boredom.

I let out a deep breath. How much trouble could I get in? I dialed Claire's cell.

"Hello?"

"Hey," I whispered, "I'm at the Hill ranch with Mom, totally bored. What are you doing?"

"Not a whole lot. Eating some Peeps, watching Melrose re-runs." I could hear her chewing. "Pretty sweet move with Mrs. Hobby's hat this morning. God, that thing was massive. She looked like she had the actual Easter Bunny copping a squat on her head."

"Yeah, that was only marginally embarrassing." I blushed remembering. "So, guess whose dad RSVP'd his son to my party?"

"Avery's?" Claire shrieked. "Yay! Now if only said party wasn't in the church basement. I don't know why your parents wouldn't take mine up on using one of the banquet rooms at the lodge. I've already reserved the Grand Ballroom for my super sweet sixteen and its eleven months away."

I sighed. "Because we'll have way less fun in a windowless wood paneled room with a concrete floor. Just another perk of being a pastor's daughter, Claire, I get an all access pass to the church rec room."

A wave of guilt washed over me the second I made that snarky comment. It was actually really nice of my parents to throw me a party. Ugh. Weirdly bitchy was taking me over today! I pulled it back to the positive. "At least there will be boys there."

"That's true." Claire paused, like she was trying to figure out how to the broach the next subject.

"Just spit it out, dude, I can sense you're waffling."

"I am indeed waffling, Zel. Um, have you considered what to do about the Melody factor?"

My parents insisted that Melody attend the party, I hadn't really thought about that one way or the other. She was my little sister, she was always there. "I haven't. You don't think she'll tattle? Wait. Do you think there'll be things worth tattling about?"

Claire giggled. "You never know."

I heard Mom round the corner into the kitchen. I slammed the phone back into its cradle, hanging up on Claire. “Ready to go, Mom?”

She gave me a suspicious look, but then let it go. “Yup, let’s move on out to the next one.”

It was almost dinner time as we drove through downtown Rosedell. Most of the buildings, faced with Old West facades, were dark. The Hitching Post gas station and drug store was still open, as was Adams Insurance. Mike Adams stood by the front window of his office, a big smile on his face, and waved when we passed by. Mom waved back, she was smiling too.

I kicked off my white scuffed flats; hand-me-down’s from Claire’s maid and put my feet up on the back of Mom’s seat. “Don’t you think it’s kinda weird that Mr. Adams is always at his office on Sunday just in time to wave to you? I mean, I know you guys are friends and all, but shouldn’t he be at home with his family?”

“Put your feet down,” Mom reached behind her and swatted at my legs. “I don’t know that it’s weird. Mike works very hard and doesn’t have the most pleasant home life. I think he spends a lot of time at his office.”

“What’s so unpleasant about his home life? Avery’s a really good student and plays a bunch of sports. His dad should be totally proud of him.” I would be proud of him if he were my kid, which is a kinda gross thing to think, but whatever.

“Oh, he is, honey. He’s very proud of him. I don’t know why I said that. Mike just works a lot.” Mom turned onto our street. “Of course, no one has as great a home life as us." She pointed to Dad and Melody as she pulled into our gravel driveway. They were engaged in the welcome home dance. Invented by my father in 2001, the welcome home dance consisted of cheesy smiles, jazz hands, hip bumps and was a Wells family tradition.

I laughed; I secretly loved the welcome home dance. "Yeah, that never gets old."

We got out of the minivan. Dad frowned, seeing that we were empty handed. "No BLT's? I'm starving!" He put his arms out and walked, stiff legged, towards Mom.

"Sorry, Pastor zombie. I thought you all were eating at the Wallaces?"

"We did. It was really good." He rubbed his belly. "You know I can always eat though."

Mom put her arm around his waist. "Yes, I know." She shepherded him up the steps and inside the house. Melody followed them, looking over her shoulder, hoping no one had seen her dancing, no doubt. I went in last, thinking how nice it was to have parents that loved each other and also that Dad had better cool it because he had a nasty bout of heartburn on the horizon.

Chapter Two

I watched Claire as she inspected her new self-inflicted haircut in the mirror stuck to the inside of her locker door. Her chin length razor-cut black hair fanned out from her face in chunky pomaded pieces. Very punk rock. Noticing a clump of bangs that was a quarter inch longer than the rest, she reached into her black patent leather tote bag and pulled a small pair of scissors from one of its many interior compartments. Grasping the disobedient clump of bangs, she snipped them off straight across.

"That's better," she said, turning her head from side to side, scrutinizing her handiwork.

"Talking to your reflection again?" I poked my head around her locker door, grabbing the magnetic mirror and holding it before my own face in mock-adoration. "Hello, beautiful!"

Claire swiped the mirror back, a grin spreading across her crimson glossed lips. "Whatever, Zellie! You know I look good!"

I spun the dial on my combination lock. "Your hair does look good. I wish I was brave enough to do something different to mine." I yanked down on the lock and opened my locker, retrieving my humongo pile of Honors English books.

"You know I would kill you if you cut your hair, it's one of your only assets," Claire joked, replacing the mirror on her locker door and slamming it shut.

"Thanks!" I linked arms with her and bumped her into the lockers with my hip, causing her tote bag to slip from her shoulder. Grace is my middle name after all. Whoops.

"Watch it now, my Amazonian friend." Claire hoisted the gigantic bag back up onto her shoulder. "We better haul ass or we're going to be late."

Mrs. Gates sat on the edge of her desk and wriggled her bifocals down to the end of her nose. She took attendance the old-fashioned way instead of passing around a sign-in sheet like all of the other teachers did. "Adams?"

Avery raised his hand. He sat in the middle of the front row. "Here."

I zoned out on him, like I always did, waiting for my name to be called at the end of attendance.

His hair was damp, curling every which way at the nape of his neck. I calculated. It'd been, what, two months since his last haircut? That seemed right. His mom probably cut it at home instead of in the salon where she worked.

I scanned the rest of him, perfection as usual. The shirt he had on today looked nice against his tan skin, a blue soccer jersey from a European team. It clung to his shoulders, riding up just a bit when he bent forward to get a pen out of his backpack. Seeing that sliver of skin gave me goose bumps. If for some crazy reason I ever got to see him with his shirt off, I was sure to hyperventilate and die right there on the spot. Yes, Jesus, I had some lust in my heart.

"Already with the staring?" Claire teased. "You know we have four other classes with him, right?"

I stuck my tongue out at her.

"Erickson?"

"Yo!" Jason said.

I tried looking at him for comparison's sake. He was decent. Blonde spiky hair. Buddy Holly glasses. Played bass in a band called...Rootie Tooty? No. Fresh and Fruity? Maybe the whole thing? I couldn't remember. He was more Claire's type. Avery's best friend and my best friend? That would be cool. I smiled, seeing Claire and Jason as plain as day engaged in a passionate argument about some indie rock band I had never heard of.

"Vargas?"

"Here." Claire saluted Mrs. Gates.

"Wells?"

"Present."

Mrs. Gates went to the blackboard and began writing. "Since we're nearing the ever so wonderful state sanctioned standardized tests, there are thirty extra vocabulary words this week. Apparently, none of you is to be left behind."

At lunch Claire chose a sundae cone from the freezer case next to the cash register and paid for it. I followed behind her in line, brownbag lunch in one hand, a thermos in the other.

We walked to our table along the back wall of the cafeteria, in closest proximity to the band and A.V. tables, but only two tables removed from where the popular kids sat. Rosedell Junior/Senior High just wasn't a big enough school for cliques to be completely separate from one another.

Claire peeled the wrapping from around her ice cream off in one clean motion.

I didn't even bother looking into my lunch bag. "Do you want any of this stuff? I don't think I can eat another peanut butter sandwich in this lifetime."

"Um, what's in the Thermos?"

"Chicken noodle."

"Nah, I'll just stick with my sugar and fat fest, thanks though." Claire looked over my shoulder. "Here comes your sister."

I crumpled down the top of my lunch bag and pushed it off to the side. Melody and three of her 7th grade friends approached our table, a whirling cloud of giggles, blonde hair, and glittery lavender nail polish.

"Hey Zel, want me to throw your lunch away too?" Melody reached out her hand, a fountain of gold bangles cascading down her arm and clinking at her wrist.

I handed the bag over. "Uh, sure." I noticed that Melody didn't have any lunch with her at all. I'm pretty sure her group of "friends" didn't eat a whole lot. "What'd you do with your Thermos?"

Melody snorted. "Yeah, like I even leave the house with that!" She glanced over her shoulder to her friends, all of them giggling in unison. "Is Mom trying to make us the lamest people in existence?"

This made me smile. "Hey, Mel, it might be too late for me, but really, save yourself now while you can."

Melody smiled back. "Duh!" She walked away, the other girls following her, and made a big show of chucking my lunch in the trashcan as she left the cafeteria.

"The rainbow and unicorn squad has left the building," Claire snarked. "I don't know how you put up with that nonsense."

"Whatever do you mean?" I asked. I was used to it. That's how Mel had always been. "Don't you know that

Melody's going to be the first popular person in our family since...well, since *my mom*!"

"You're right, how stupid of me to even ask."

Principal Landry came into the cafeteria and walked over to the table where Avery was sitting with Jason, a few seniors from the baseball team, and several girls on the student council and in cheerleading.

"Avery, your mom is on the phone asking to speak with you immediately. Would you come to my office please?"

A chorus of "ooh's" and "what did you do now's" erupted from the table. A blush like wildfire covered Avery's face. He shrugged his shoulders as if to say "how do I know?" and followed principal Landry.

"What do you think that was about?" I asked. I felt really cruddy that Avery was so embarrassed. I knew it totally sucked to have everyone staring at you.

Claire leaned towards me and lowered her voice. "Well...I don't know for certain, but my mom has told me about Avery's mom getting drunk in one of the bars at the lodge a couple of times. The bartenders have had to call him to come pick her up. I guess it could be that."

Claire's parents owned and operated the largest ski resort in the area. It housed a grand lodge, several fine dining restaurants, and three bars. Half the people in Rosedell worked there. She was privy to a lot of the gossip in town because of it.

"But why would she call Avery?" I asked. "He doesn't even have his license yet. Why wouldn't Mr. Adams pick her up?"

"Probably because Mr. Adams is a tool."

"Yeah, I can see that. Huh. That totally sucks for Avery though." I lowered my voice too. "Y'know, Mr.

Adams was at his office window again yesterday when we were driving home. He's been there every Sunday for the past few months."

"Ick. Do you think he's stalking your mom or something?"

"Nah. I mean, they're friends. She did say that he worked so much because he had an 'unpleasant home life,' whatever that means. Maybe she was talking about Avery's mom?" I opened the Thermos, yup, chicken noodle, just as I suspected. I poured some soup into the lid and drank it.

"Didn't they used to be friends too? His mom and yours? Wish you knew what happened there." Claire helped herself to the next cup of soup that I poured.

"Mom never wants to talk about it. All she'll say is that Avery and I were so cute when we used to play together. Then he went to kindergarten and she wanted to try home-schooling me--"

"Thank God that didn't last!"

"Seriously? It's not bad enough that I'm a pastor's daughter and live in a small town surrounded by mountains?"

Claire nodded. "How would I have ever survived 5th grade without you? The second we moved to Rose-hell I was ready to go back to boarding school." She reached across the table and took my hands in hers. "Then I saw you on the playground, wearing those high-water orange corduroys and I knew that dorkiness would be our bond."

"I loved those pants!" I said, slapping her hands away.

I chugged the rest of the soup straight from the Thermos and then screwed the lid back on. Soup dribbled down the sides.

Claire handed me a napkin. "C'mon, I gotta pee and fix my face before French. I'll get the lowdown on what happened from my mom tonight. See if Mrs. Adams was even at the lodge."

Avery nodded at the bartender as he hurried over to the stage in the corner of the lounge. His mom stood stock still in the middle, microphone in hand, belting out "Memories" from CATS. She liked to get loaded and re-live her high school theater geek days. The few other tipsy people in the place cheered her on.

He reached out a hand to her. "Mom, I'm here to pick you up. Let's go!"

She stopped singing and stumbled forward, bracing herself on her son's shoulders. "Avery! Honey! What are you doing here?"

"You called me to come get you. Out of school?" He sighed, exasperated. "You called me out of school to come and pick you up. Don't you remember? It was like, half an hour ago."

She pulled away from him. "But I'm just getting started, honey! I'm having so much fun! Let me do one more, please? You know my Evita is so good."

Avery stepped up onto the stage and took the microphone from her hand. An audience member booed him. "No, Mom, c'mon, I gotta get back to school. I have to get Jason's truck back to him."

"Oh, all right," she took a bow and then gestured toward Avery, "my son, ladies and gentlemen!" The same guy booed again.

He put his arm around her waist and helped her down from the stage. On the way out, he grabbed a to-go cup of coffee the bartender handed him. "Thanks again, Tom."

Out in the parking lot his mom squinted her eyes in the early afternoon sun. "Jesus, it's bright out here! What time did you say it was again?"

"It's one in the afternoon, Mom. You called while I was at lunch."

She giggled. "And how embarrassing was that for you?"

"Pretty freaking embarrassing."

Avery opened the passenger side door to Jason's pickup and helped his mom in, buckling her seat belt. "I thought we agreed that you were only going to do this sort of thing after work with co-workers who can legally drive you home."

Tears welled up in her eyes. "Oh, honey! I'm so sorry! I don't know what I was thinking. What an idiot I am."

He got into the truck and wiped the tears from his mom's face with his shirtsleeve. "It's okay. You've just gotta be more careful. If Dad finds out about this...well you know that won't be good."

They sat in silence on the way home. His mom dozed off. He pulled into the driveway, getting as close to the garage as he could and hopped out, punching in the code for the door. As soon as it started opening he went around to his mom's side and helped her out of the truck. He got her into the garage as quickly as possible. He didn't think any of the neighbors had seen them, this time anyway.

After he got his mom out of her shoes and into bed, and a large glass of water on the bedside table, he jogged out to the truck and headed back to school.

What had Zellie thought of him, leaving school in the middle of the day? He was sure that Claire had filled her in on why his mom needed him. She was wasted in Claire's parents' place of business, after all.

To distract himself, Avery thought of Zellie in church the day before, knocking that big hat off of Mrs. Hobby's head. Hilarious. Classic Zellie. She was always acting like a goof and looking beautiful doing it. He'd tried to get in on the joke with her, smile at her during communion, but she had just made the weirdest face and turned away from him. Then, during the sermon she was leaning forward and it seemed like she was looking his way, but she must have been looking past him.

She was so confusing, more so than any other girl he knew. Not that he had vast experience to draw on or anything. For the most part, he'd just been on group outings to the movies, stuff like that. No other girl made him as nervous or as unsure of himself as Zellie did.

Many things came easily for him. Grades, sports, friendships, and he probably could've had his pick of a few really cool girls, but none of them...shook him up like her. When they were younger and he had more of a grip on his feelings, Avery had been able to push down whatever it was about Zellie that mesmerized him. The past couple of years, though, he could not keep his eyes off of her. Could not keep himself from wondering what it would take to make her happy. Could not stop himself from imagining and staring and being so into her. It was probably going to kill him.

After parking Jason's pickup where it was that morning, Avery jogged into the school, careful to avoid the office. He hadn't exactly told Mr. Landry that he was going to pick up his mom.

Chapter Three

"Zellie, I was thinking about taking a trip over to Bend on Saturday to get some decorations for your party. Do you want to come with me or do you trust me to pick them out myself?" Dad said, as he scooped a large helping of green beans onto his plate already piled high with fried chicken and rice.

I took the green bean bowl from him and flicked a few onto my plate. "I'd like to go. Can Claire come too?"

"And Melody?" Melody chimed in.

"It would be fine if Claire came with us. Melody, I seem to remember you have math tutoring with Mrs. Kent."

"Dad! That is so not fair. I'm totally getting a C- in math and do not need help. Please, I really wanna go."

Dad stabbed a forkful of beans. "Perhaps you could see if Mrs. Kent would move tutoring to Friday evening? Then you could come with us."

Melody kicked the table leg. "Well, that won't work either because I'm supposed to go to Britney's slumber party on Friday. Can't I skip tutoring just this one time?"

"Not the first time, sweetie," Mom said.

Melody pushed back from the table and ran into the bedroom that we shared.

Dad chuckled. "That's about how I thought that would go."

"Yup," I answered, grinning.

"Be nice you two. You know she doesn't like it when you all do things without her." Mom went to the bedroom to comfort her.

"What do you think Zel, leave around 10? Tell Claire we'll pick her up."

"Sounds good. Could I maybe also look for a dress to wear?" I really didn't want to spend my sweet sixteen birthday wearing hand-me-downs or churchy clothes. If I was ever going to have any chance of getting Avery to talk to me, I had to a least attempt to look hot. "I'm sure I can find something good on sale," I added.

Dad gave me a wink. "I don't see why not. You're only sixteen once!"

After Claire had agreed to go to Bend, the rest of the school week raced by and for once I had something to look forward to on the weekend besides church.

On Friday afternoon I stood out in front of the school waiting for Mom to pick me up and take me to my dentist appointment like I was an 8-year-old. I couldn't wait to take Driver's Ed in the summer, driving was going to be, well, freedom.

It was a windy spring day and my hair was blowing all over the place, creating a whirlwind around my head. Annoyed, I grabbed my unruly mass of hair in both hands and slicked it back, rolling a ponytail holder from my wrist onto the loose, messy twist I'd made at the base of my skull.

"You missed a chunk." Avery reached over and tucked the hair behind my ear.

I froze, paralyzed. Avery had just touched me. I felt myself go tomato red and shiver at the same time. Was I awake? I traced the path of his fingers across my cheekbone, re-tucking the hair behind my ear, stalling. "Oh," I said brilliantly.

He stood next to me, straddling his bike; like it was something we did every day. Like he had spoken to me once in the past five years. Like he acknowledged my presence. His beautiful long fingers had a firm grip on the handle bars.

"So that practice test in English totally sucked, don't you think?" he said.

A hundred images flashed through my mind. His full lips, his hair curling over his ears, the sliver of skin that had given me goose bumps. I had to pull myself together! I had to speak. I had to not go catatonic. "Yeah," I managed to say. "It completely sucked. Way sucked. Can't imagine how much the real test is going to totally...suck." I completely, way, and totally needed to cease talking for the rest of my miserable existence.

"Totally," he agreed, giving me a crinkly-eyed smile.

We loitered in awkward silence for what seemed like forever. I finally turned towards him to espouse some more of my wisdom, when a strong gust of wind blew past us, unleashing my crazy hair from my ponytail, and blowing it right into his face. I rushed to smooth it back again, but Avery grasped my wrist.

"It's cool. It's not bothering me." He rubbed his thumb up along the inside my palm. "Your hair is really soft. It's nice."

"Oh!" I said brilliantly again. "Uh, thanks. Yours is too." Shut up. Shut up now. Pray like you've never prayed before that an angel seamstress will come down from heaven and sew your mouth shut!

He let go of my wrist, but the warmth from his hand lingered. I resisted putting my arm to my nose, curious if I could smell him on my skin.

He ran his hands through his hair. "So, your party is next week. That's cool."

"Yeah," I said, attempting to be nonchalant. As if. "Claire and I are going to Bend with my dad to get decorations and stuff tomorrow."

"Sweet, Bend's cool."

"Yeah!" I. Am. So. Super. Excited! Holy Christ on a cracker why couldn't I say one intelligent thing?

"Well, uh, all righty." He looked at the watch he had hooked to his backpack. "Um, I gotta get over to my dad's office. Have fun in Bend. I'll see you in church...and then y'know in school on Monday."

"Yeah! I'll see you on Sunday and Monday!" The embarrassment was becoming debilitating.

I watched as he rode away, not sure of what just happened or of anything that I had said. Was I already at the dentist, because I sure as hell felt like I was on laughing gas? This would've been another opportune moment to have a cell phone. I had to call Claire as soon as I got home. There was so much to analyze. There was *something* to analyze!

Avery rode his bike down Cascade Ave. How many times had he just said "cool?" Ugh. Too many. Well, at least she'd talked to him. Sort of. He was having a hard time actually remembering what they'd talked about in between all the times he'd said cool. *I am such a massive dork.*

This was all Jason's fault. Avery had been perfectly fine admiring Zellie from afar, checking her out on the sly during youth group. Every day he looked forward to 6th period Humanities, the one class where they had a reverse alphabetical seating chart and he sat behind her, allowing him to fantasize about gently sweeping her hair to the side and kissing her neck.

Staring and wanting and longing were things he was comfortable with, but Jason said he was acting like a little girl. When he had threatened to tell Zellie that Avery was in love with her if he didn't at least say hi to her before her birthday party, Avery could've killed him. But, he had to admit, it had gone better than he thought it would.

Oh God, he couldn't believe he'd touched her. Twice. Where did that impulse come from? Fear of exposure had made him brave. He wished he could have held onto to her wrist forever. She hadn't pulled away from him either, so that was saying something. Ugh. What was that saying? That she was being polite? That she'd wanted him to touch her? He hadn't really given her a choice. It seemed like it was okay with her. It was okay. Everything was cool. Ugh!

Skidding to a stop on the sidewalk in front of his dad's insurance office, he hopped off his bike and propped it up against the building. Every day after school when he didn't have practice or a game he had to help his dad at work. He did the crappy jobs, like emptying the trash and cleaning out the coffee pot, while his friends got to hang out at each other's houses and play video games.

The cow bell clanked as Avery walked through the glass door that read "Adams Insurance" in curly old fashioned script.

His dad looked up from his desk, near the back wall of the small storefront. "Did you lock up your bike or leave it out there so that anyone walking by could take it for a spin?"

Avery flung his backpack down on the floor next to the old black leather sofa that used to be in their living room at home. It now occupied the "waiting area" in his dad's office, even though it was only about five feet from his desk. "No one's gonna take it, Dad." Avery flopped onto the sofa, slouching down low so that his dad had to look over the stack of files on his desk to see him.

"This may be a small town, but that doesn't mean that bad things don't happen. If that were the case, I'd be out of a job. Go lock it up." He finished filling out a stack of forms he had been working on and tossed them into his "out" box.

Avery rose from the couch with incredible slowness, as if moving at a more reasonable pace would kill him.

"All right Mr. Wiseass, instead of locking up your bike why don't you go pick up our suits from the dry cleaners." His dad shifted forward in his chair and pulled his wallet out of the back pocket of his khakis.

Avery froze in mid-sloth. "Why are our suits at the dry cleaners? Did someone die?"

"No, someone did not die. I thought we should look nice for Zellie Wells' birthday party next weekend. Plus, it's been awhile since we've had our suits cleaned." He flipped a twenty toward his son. It floated in the space between them for a split second and then fell at Avery's feet.

He bent down and picked it up, cramming it into his jeans pocket. "Why do I have to wear a suit, anyways? I'm going to look like a total dork. Jason's dad isn't going to make him--"

"Jason's dad doesn't make him do anything and that's why Jason is a spoiled brat. You are wearing a suit because you're going to be in church and because I'm wearing a suit. End of discussion. You better get over there. They close early on Fridays."

Avery grabbed his backpack and slung it over his left shoulder. "How am I supposed to carry two suits on my bike?"

"You'll think of something." He pulled a stack of papers from his "in" box and began filling them out.

Avery made it to the dry cleaners just before closing and was now trying for the third time to ride his bike home without destroying the suits or himself. Steadying the bike with one hand and holding the suits up as high as he could with the other he attempted to pedal. The stupid plastic dry cleaning bags kept getting wrapped up in the spokes of his back wheel, throwing him off balance and shredding the bottoms of the bags.

"Damn it!" He threw the suits to the ground, sprang from his bike and walked away from the whole mess, leaving his bike and the suits lying in the middle of the empty residential street.

He sat down on the curb. He could not wait until he turned sixteen in July, no more running errands on his lousy bike!

"I couldn't help but notice what a total jackass you were making of yourself. Wanna use my phone to call your mom?"

Claire was standing above him holding out her red glittery cell phone.

"Thanks. That would be really cool." Avery cringed at his words. He took the phone from Claire and dialed the number to Clear Cuts, the hair salon where his mom worked. "Yeah, hi, Juanita, it's Avery, can I talk to my mom please."

"Oh, hi, sweetie!" Juanita said, her high pitched fake southern accent dripping with honey. "Let me get her...Becky, that adorable little son of yours is on the phone. Here she comes, sugar."

"Thanks." Avery listened as Juanita laid the phone down. It slid off the reception desk and bounced on the floor. He heard his mom say "Oh shit!" and then "Sorry! Pardon my French."

His mom giggled into the phone. "Hi, honey, is everything okay?"

"Uh, yeah, Dad sent me to pick up our suits from the dry cleaners and I'm having a really hard time getting them home on my bike. Could you come pick me up? I'm sitting on the curb in front of Claire Vargas' house."

Avery turned and looked up. Claire was hovering over him reciting her address. Avery put his hand over the phone. "Everyone knows where you live Claire. Shhhh!"

She stopped talking and sat down next to him on the curb.

"Why the hell would your father have you pick up those suits on your bike? I swear sometimes I don't know what goes through that man's head. Of course I'll come get you. It's only fair, right?" His mom giggled again, more embarrassed this time. "I'm just finishing up with Mrs. Tucker. I'll be over in a few minutes, okay?"

"Okay, Mom. Thanks. See you in a few minutes." Avery handed the phone back to Claire. "She'll be here in a few minutes."

"So I hear." Claire stood up from the curb, tugging her bright blue mini skirt down in an attempt to cover the stippled impression on the backs of her legs. "Do you want to come inside and have a pop or something?"

Avery stood up. "Yeah, okay, let me just get all my crap out of the street." He walked over to the bike and dragged it and the tangled up suits into the Vargas' impeccably landscaped yard. He followed her into her house, a huge remodeled Victorian, probably one of the first houses built in Rosedell.

Avery liked Claire. Not that they had ever really been close friends or anything, but they had known each other for awhile and she was pretty funny for a girl.

Jason always said that Claire liked him and wanted to get in his pants, but Avery didn't see her that way. Besides, she was Zellie's best friend and he couldn't risk messing up his chances with Zellie. That is, if he had a chance with her.

He did want to know if Zellie liked him, but it wasn't like he could come right out and ask Claire if she did. He knew Claire would just tell her. Then what if she didn't like him? He didn't know if he could stand it. He had spent so long liking Zellie and not doing anything about it, playing it safe, that he was used to not knowing. He hung out in the front hall while Claire went into the kitchen and got them each a pop.

She opened the cans and set them on the granite countertop of the island. "You can come in here, y'know. My parents aren't home."

Avery sat down at the island.

"So," Claire began, "you excited about Zellie's party next weekend?"

He shifted on the bar stool. "Um, yeah, it should be fun. Zellie's cool."

Claire leaned further toward him, "Oh you think so, do you?"

"Sure, yeah, I guess." He took a long drink of his pop.

She walked around the island and hoisted herself up onto the barstool next to him. "Interesting."

He tried his hardest to be nonchalant. "Whatever."

"Nice try, dude, but I can see right through you." She nudged him in the ribs with her elbow. "You better ask her to dance at her party. If you wait too long someone else is going to come along and snap her up. She's not going to wait forever, you know."

Avery looked down at the countertop, too shocked to make eye contact with Claire. How clueless was he? "Does everyone know I like her?"

She chugged her pop, taking a long time to answer, and then let out an enormous belch. "Everyone but her, dude."

"Can we keep it that way until next weekend? I promise I will make a move," he pleaded. "Awesome belch by the way."

Claire smiled. "Thank you. I aim to please." She poked him in the chest, warning. "I'll keep your secret, but if you don't tell her soon, I'm going to. Watching the two of you pine after each other is getting ridiculous."

Avery suddenly felt very hot. "So, she likes me too?"

Claire hopped down off the barstool, "Your mom's here."

He looked toward the front door. "How did you know that?"

"Uh, the doorbell rang. Wow. You really are a lost cause." Claire pulled Avery from his barstool and pushed him toward the front door, "See ya at youth group, lover boy."

"See you. Thanks for letting me use your phone."

The phone rang in my hand just as I was about to call Claire. "Hello?" I answered.

"You will not believe who was just at my house!" Claire squealed.

I heard her fling herself onto the leather sectional in her family room. Uh, oh, this was sure to be a long conversation. "Hey! I was just about to call you. Um, let me go into my room. Hold on."

I walked down the hall, shut my bedroom door, and plopped on my twin bed. "So, *you* will not believe what happened to me after school!"

"It cannot be as good as what just happened here--"

"Avery!" was the first word we both said. After that we talked over each other for a good three seconds.

"Wait. What?" Claire said. "He talked to you! What did he say? Tell me everything!"

"He was in your house! *You* tell me everything!" I got up from my bed and started to pace around the room. These developments were too exciting to be lying down.

"Okay, so he was trying to ride his bike and carry dry cleaning at the same time."

"Why did he have dry cleaning? What was it?" I needed absolutely every detail.

"Well, from what I gather, it was the suit that he is going to wear to your birthday party. So, anyways, the bag kept getting caught in his wheels and he got all mad and threw a fit. I went outside to do some recon. I pretended to get the mail and there he was sitting on the curb in front of my house, so I asked him if he needed to borrow my phone."

"Oh, my God." Claire was so brave, she could talk to hot boys like they were normal people.

"Yeah, so he calls his mom and she couldn't come pick him up for a few minutes, so I invited him inside for a pop."

"Oh, my God. What kind?"

"Of pop? Coke. So then I ask him about your party and if he's looking forward to it and he said that he was and that you're cool!"

"He thinks I'm cool? No freaking way!" I felt like I was going to pass out. "What else did he say?"

"Zellie, I think there's a very good chance that Avery is going to ask you to dance at your party." Claire giggled.

"I will totally die!" I would, I totally would. "Do you think he really will?"

"Yes, for sure, I could almost guarantee it. So what happened after school? What's up with all of this Avery interaction?"

"Well," I took in a deep breath, "I was standing over by the bike racks waiting for my mom to pick me up and he just like, appeared next to me! It was super windy and my hair was blowing everywhere and I pulled it back, but missed a little and he--"

Mom peeked her head in the door. "I need your help with dinner."

I nodded and then pointed to the phone. She nodded back and closed the door. "Crap. My mom needs help with dinner. I'll have to tell you the rest tomorrow."

"I can't wait!" Claire said, "I'll see you at ten."

Claire climbed into the back of our decrepit blue minivan in as ladylike a manner as she could while wearing a denim miniskirt. I could hardly keep a straight face watching her. Grace was her middle name as well. Okay, Graciella, but still. "I think it might be time to invest in some skorts my friend."

She snorted. "Oh, I think you've got that market covered Corduroy. Hey, Pastor Paul."

"Good morning. I trust your parents know that we're going to Bend today?" he said into the rearview mirror.

Claire slammed the van door shut. "Yup. I left them a note."

Dad popped a Rolling Stones cassette into the ancient tape player as we made our way out of town. It was either that or Gospel Elvis and the drive to Bend was desolate and ranch laden. Some tunage was a must.

The minivan creaked and moaned as we drove into the parking lot of Party Depot, and then shuddered when Dad turned off the ignition.

"Are you sure this thing is still going to be drivable by the time I get my license?" I asked. We all got out.

Dad shut his door, not even bothering to lock it. "I'm just hoping it lasts you through Driver's Ed this summer. I don't think it'll be making too many more out of town trips." He kicked the front tire. "So, I thought we'd get the decorations here and then head over to the mall and look at some dresses. Sound good?"

I gave him a knowing smile, thankful he hadn't forgotten about a new dress. "Sounds good."

After we left the Party Depot with two big bags crammed full of decorations in my fave colors, pink and green, we stopped at the food court in the mall for pizza. When we were finished consuming eleventy billion calories, Dad handed me three twenties.

"Sorry it can't be more, honey."

I gave him a hug and a quick kiss on the cheek. "It's plenty. Thank you." It totally was. I figured he'd been putting stuff on the emergency credit card to even be able to give me sixty bucks. Sale dresses here I come!

"You girl's have fun dress shopping. I'll be in Kitchen Kaboodle perusing the latest Barefoot Contessa."

"Thanks again, Dad."

He gave me a wink and went on his way.

"Alone at long last!" Claire said, linking her arm with mine and dragging me into Macy's. "I want to know every second of everything that happened with Avery."

I blushed spastically and made a beeline for the sales rack in the Juniors Department. "He...I can't believe he actually did this, but like I was saying yesterday, my hair was blowing all around and he reached up and tucked it behind my ear and then I had no idea what to do next, but he just stayed put." I pulled a lavender shift from the rack, holding it up for Claire's opinion. She crinkled her nose. I threw the dress over my arm anyway and flipped through the rack some more. "I think we talked about the English practice test...I vaguely remember saying how much it sucked like eighty-two times. What about this green one?" Claire nodded her head yes. I eyed the rack. A lot of the dresses were too fancy; probably for prom. "I think these two are good, come with me while I try them on."

We walked into the dressing room. Claire sat on a chair in the corner and held the dresses. "So..."

I yanked my shirt off over my head. "Then, I have no idea why I did this, I sort of turned toward him like this," I turned, "and my hair was blowing right in his face, practically up his nose! It was totally embarrassing. But then I tried to pull my hair back again and he grabbed my wrist and told me not to!"

"What? Why?" Claire took the lavender dress off the hanger and handed it to me.

"This is my favorite part!" I stepped into the dress and turned so Claire could zip it up. "He said that it wasn't bothering him and that he thought my hair was nice!"

Claire zipped the dress up. "Oh, my God!"

"I know, right? What do you think it means?" I looked at myself in the mirror, also crinkling my nose at this dress. Yuck-o-rama, I looked deadish. I turned back around and Claire unzipped it.

A quiet chuckle escaped from the next dressing room.

My eyes met with Claire's and we burst out in laughter. Sometimes we got way out of hand with our "oh my god's" and "totally's". We did actually have brains in our heads.

The door to the other dressing room opened. We stuck our heads out of the room and saw a well dressed older lady with grey streaked auburn hair and an enormous brown leather pocketbook.

"Sorry we were being so obnoxious!" Claire called, "I guess you couldn't help but hear us."

The lady looked back. "You two remind me of my daughter and her best friend when they were teenagers." She smiled at us and then walked out into the store.

We ducked back into the dressing room. I held the lavender dress out to Claire and took the green one from the hanger, sliding it on. It flowed over my body, grazing all the right areas, brightening up the color of my eyes.

Claire grinned. "That's the one Zel. How much is it?"

I pulled the tag out from under my armpit. I hadn't even bothered to look earlier. "$59.99, it was meant to be."

Chapter Four

In youth group on Sunday, I hoped that Avery would talk to me again, but all he offered up was a kind "hello." Had I been reading too much into our conversation on Friday? Claire, too? As we had proven at the mall, we were prone to being spazmatic and teenagery when it came to him. Maybe Avery was just being nice. That was probably it. I was such a dork, standing there letting my generic shampoo smelling hair blow up his nose. What's that smell? Oh, eau de pathetic Jesus home-school girl? Check ya later. Ugh.

The school week dragged on, more of the same, practice tests and peanut butter sandwiches. By Saturday, my birthday, I was ready to bust out of my skin. Avery or no Avery, I was finally sixteen. Thank freakin' God.

"I'm not really sure if I want to put the streamers up, Dad. What do you think? Does it seem too, uh, juvenile?" I stood in the middle of the church basement, surveying the pink and green streamers that Dad had spent the better part of an hour twisting and affixing around the room, dragging his ladder from corner to corner.

"Honey, streamers are not juvenile. I had them at my fortieth birthday party in this very room, don't you remember?" Dad ripped a strip of tape from the dispenser he had tucked under his arm and secured the last length of streamer above the door to his office.

"The ones you had at your birthday were black, Dad. It was a joke. Don't *you* remember *old* man?" I smiled and ran to him, hugging his legs. The streamers looked beautiful, whether they were juvenile or not.

Dad put his hand on my head and ruffled up my hair.

"Hey!" I pulled away from him, smoothing my hair back down. I had already washed it for the day and wasn't going to have an hour to wash and blow-dry it again.

"Just wait 'til your mom and I are outta here before you and your friends decide to rip them down, okay?" He climbed from the ladder, folded it up and stowed it in his office. He stooped under the doorway. "All right kiddo," he said, ducking back out of his office. "Let's get you home so you can get gussied up."

Claire and Melody were already dressed for the party and waiting for me in the family room.

I came rushing through the front door and went directly into Claire's open arms.

"Oh, my God!!!" We screamed, as if we had not seen each other twenty-four hours before or hadn't talked on the phone six times already that day.

Dad walked through the front door carrying an armload of extra party decorations. "Girls, taking the Lord's name in vain...do I need to remind you?"

"Sorry, Dad."

"Sorry, Pastor Paul." We both lowered our eyes, becoming very interested in our feet. OMG was a hard habit to break, I was usually better at switching my real vernacular and my parental vernacular on or off depending on who I was with.

Dad smiled, dumping the bags on the faded green couch next to Melody, who was sitting perfectly still as to not wrinkle her dress. “I know you’re excited, let’s just keep the commandment breaking to a minimum this evening.”

“Okay, Dad. C’mon!” I grabbed Claire by the hand and dragged her down the hall to my room.

She pushed a pile of stuffed animals from Melody’s bed and plopped on it. Her red mini skirt rode up, only just covering her thighs. “So, what did you decide to do with your hair?”

“I’m going to put it up,” I said, while simultaneously pulling my t-shirt off with one hand, unbuttoning my shorts with the other and kicking my flip flops into the closet. I had to be quick with the undress. It was gonna take some time to get me to the hotness level I desired.

“Cool. You are going to look so cool.” Claire rolled to her side and propped her head up with her hand. “I brought a bunch of hair products and eye shadow and stuff. Avery isn’t going to know what hit him.”

“Let’s hope not.” I shimmied the pale green slip dress over my head.

After arriving at the church with my family and Claire, I started getting a sinking feeling in the pit of my stomach that I was about to have the lamest sixteen-year-old birthday party ever. Once inside, as all of the guests and their parents began to arrive, my feelings were confirmed.

A few girls from youth group, along with Claire and Melody, huddled around me in one corner of the church basement. Everyone else stood next to their parents, who were all busy kissing up to my dad. One of the five people

I'd invited that didn't go to church with me showed up. I was not feeling the love.

Avery hovered behind his dad, his hands shoved into the pockets of his gray slacks, twisting his neck from side to side trying to loosen his tie. Mr. Adams was wearing his Sunday suit and whispering something into my mom's ear. She laughed loud enough for the whole room to hear and put her hand on his shoulder.

Mortified was the exact word that I would use to describe my exact feeling at that exact moment. "I am seriously going to die. What is this, a pancake breakfast or a birthday party? Everyone's parents made them wear church clothes!" I looked at Claire, hoping that perhaps I was overreacting.

She winced. "Okay, girl, we've just got to get through the cake and then all the parental units will leave and the real party can begin. We've got a stereo, I made you an awesome compilation...and you look hot. Avery will be slow dancing with his hands on your butt in no time. Trust me."

I grinned. Claire must know something she wasn't telling me. I could feel my self confidence returning. Looking past her, I peeked at Avery, who happened to be staring right at me and grinning too. "Melody, tell Mom to bring the cake out now."

"Happy Birthday, honey! We'll be back around eleven to pick you girls up. Have fun and behave." Mom leaned down and gave both me and Mel a kiss on the cheek. "Call us on the phone in your dad's office if anything happens and you need us, okay?"

"Everything will be fine Mom, get out of here!" I waved goodbye to my well-intentioned parents from my seat at a long wooden table.

With that, all of the adult energy was sucked out of the room. Cell phones were flipped open, ties hung on the backs of folding chairs, and twin sets lost their cardigan components. The room full of teenagers relaxed and gave a concerted sigh of relief.

Claire went to the stereo and put on the compilation, a fast song began playing. "The fun portion of the party will begin now," she announced. Walking over to Jason, she took his cell phone from his hands, flipped it shut and slipped it deep into his pants pockets. "Care for a dance, sailor?"

I laughed, but remained glued to my metal folding chair. Claire's capacity for saving me through her own personal embarrassment was limitless, thank God.

People began pairing off to dance in the middle of the concrete basement floor. That left me and Melody sitting at one end of the table and Avery and Ricky Sykes at the other. The dancing couples were oblivious to us four awkward people inspecting our cuticles at the table.

I poked Melody in the arm. She totally owed me for being allowed at my party. I could have banned her with enough whining to Dad. "Mel, go ask Ricky to dance."

Melody continued picking the nail polish from her fingers. She gave a sideways glance at the short and zitty Ricky Sykes. "Ick. He's like three years older than me and four inches shorter. Why would I want to dance with him?"

I got to my feet. She was never going to change, what did I expect? "Fine, be that way. I'm going to dance." Out of the corner of my eye I could see that when I stood up, Avery had too. Crap! I needed to ask him to dance before he could flee, which is what I was now sure he wanted to do. Instead, he walked over to me.

I turned toward him, trying not to pass out or throw up.

"Hey, Zellie, uh, happy birthday." He ran his fingers through his hair. I could never get tired of watching him do that.

His deep brown eyes looked into mine. Passing out was becoming more and more of a realistic possibility by the minute.

"Thanks, Avery," I managed to say, balancing myself with one hand on the edge of the table.

He mimed his hands on a steering wheel, motioning like he was driving a car. "Sixteen. Cool." His face went red and he stuck his hands into his pockets.

I put my hands on the invisible steering wheel too. "Yeah! Driving. I'm taking Driver's Ed this summer. Should be pretty awesome." Oh, my God. Because waking up at six in the morning and sweating in a car full of other nervous kids is pretty awesome? I grabbed onto the table again. I didn't have pockets. "Your birthday's in July if I remember, right?" His birthday was July third. I'd practically been born knowing that, but I didn't want to seem like a stalker.

"Yeah, July third, it's pretty cool...y'know with the 4th and all. There's usually a rodeo."

"That's a great birthday! Fun. I like the rodeo. Horses...in the corral? The clowns? Funny." I had not been to the rodeo since I was like eight. What the hell was I talking about?

"So, um, cool party, Miss Zellie...who is sixteen." He reached out and gave me a playful punch on the arm.

"Oh, no, it's not, but thanks for saying so." I shrugged my shoulders, relaxing my death grip on the edge of the table and attempting to slyly graze my hand up my arm to the spot where he had touched me.

"My dad made me wear a suit." He jammed his hands back into his pockets.

He seemed a little nervous too. That made me feel better. Avery Adams gets nervous talking to me. "Yeah, I see that. You look really hot though. Like good, nice, not...the opposite of cold." I felt a sudden tingle of warmth throughout my body. I crossed my arms across my breasts as the tingle obviously passed through them. Yikes, for once I'd rather blush.

Avery glanced down at my chest, breaking eye contact for the first time since we started talking. He was totally looking at my nipples! "You look really pretty." Avery's eyes locked back on mine.

Aw, screw it. I lowered my arms back down to my sides, speechless. I kinda didn't care if the whole room was scoping my nips at this point; I was filled with reckless sixteen-year-old abandon.

"Jesus H. Christ, Avery," Claire shouted from the "dance floor" that was now more of an open space for the couples to rhythmically grope one another, "ask the girl to dance already! She's going to be a virgin until she's twenty at this rate!"

"Thanks, Claire!" I called back to her, a crimson blush overtaking my whole face.

"Well," Avery said, taking my sweaty palm in his, "we wouldn't want that to happen." His eyes got wide and he started to backpedal. "Not that...virginity is good. I'm good with it...too?" He took a deep breath in and then blew it out slowly. "Let's just dance. This song is really good. Jason's band Fresh and Fruity covers it."

As Avery's fingers intertwined with mine, a jolt of electricity shot through me. I could feel my blood circulating through my body, whooshing in and out of my heart. All of my senses became hyperaware. The smell of pine overwhelmed me. A million flashes of Avery went through my mind. His mouth, his hair, his hand now in mine and then a vision of the future played out behind my eyes.

Avery covered in blood, an older version of himself, splayed out on the side of the road. He was next to a red pickup truck with its driver's side smashed in. I was there too, older, screaming, holding my pregnant belly, kneeling down beside him.

"Hey, are you okay?" Avery asked.

I blinked hard and the vision disappeared. He was still holding my hand. How long had I spaced out for? It couldn't have been long.

"Yeah, I'm fine." What the hell just happened? I was so not fine. Why was I ruining this for myself? I had to pull it together. "Blecch!" I shook my head and stuck out my tongue, "I just spaced for a moment, sorry! Let's dance, please. This song is good." I had no freakin' idea what song was playing.

He led me to the center of the room. I could feel everyone's eyes on us.

"I'm glad it's a slow song," he said, "I don't really know how to dance."

Oh, good. Slow dancing. Much, much easier. "Yeah, I can't dance very well either." I pictured myself doing the welcome home dance. That evened me out a little. I tentatively put my hands on his shoulders.

He put his hands on my hips at first, and then instead, moved them to the small of my back, pulling me closer to him. It seemed it was his turn to be filled with reckless sixteen-year-old abandon. We rocked back and forth. I suppose you could call it dancing.

Despite the whole vision thing, which I was completely choosing to block out until later, I expected to be freaking out a lot more in Avery's arms than I was. He felt comfortable, right.

I let my hands glide from his shoulders towards the nape of his neck. This was my real freak out test. I took hold of a lock of his hair and rubbed it between my fingers. It was so soft, like satin. Okay, that wasn't very manly. It was like...how it was supposed to be. How I had dreamt it would feel. I was glad his mom hadn't cut it after all.

The music changed. It got faster, then slower. Again and again. We stayed as we were. I didn't care about the other people in the room. What they thought of me, if they thought of me. He was it. Avery was the only thing in my mind. I looked into his eyes. I trusted him, felt close to him. We drifted into the corner.

He leaned into me, backing me up against the wall. And just like I'd pictured a hundred times, he rested his forehead against mine.

"I'm going to kiss you now," he said.

My heart jumped in my chest. The breath from his words was hot on my lips. I gulped, moving my mouth closer to his. "Okay," was all I could say. I had no idea what I was doing. I was just gonna go with it.

The instant Avery pulled my top lip in between his, my anxiety melted away, and was replaced by sensory overload. Every ounce of my body pulsed.

He pressed against me closer, harder, pushing his mouth into mine. I grabbed at him, sliding my hands under his jacket, drawing him to me. There wasn't thought. My body acted independently of my brain, out of my control. I arched my back, meeting his touch at every point of contact.

I breathed him in, finally. He smelled sweet and clean, like oranges and...Glycerin soap. My lips were going numb.

"You okay?" he asked, coming up for air. "I'm, uh, that was even better than I thought it would be."

"Keep going." I brought my swollen mouth up to his.

He traced the edge of my face with his nose, kissing my neck. I thought I was going to spontaneously combust. I twisted my fingers into his hair, pulling his mouth back to mine. His fingertips brushed up and down my waist. He moved his hands around to the small of my back, grasping my hips. I didn't push him away. I wanted this.

Then Melody was saying something and everyone was hurrying around the room. Different, faster music put on. We stood there stunned, looking into each other's eyes, letting the intensity move between us for just a second more. Avery backed away from me. He looked like he'd been punched in the mouth.

"Tomorrow, after church, can you meet me at the lake?"

I almost couldn't get the words out of my own puffy lips. "Yes. Yeah. I'll be there."

Avery felt electric. Lying on top of his made bed in the dark, still wearing his church clothes, he listened for his parents, trying to detect any movement coming from their bedroom. All he could hear was the energy coming off of him. The whole room was buzzing.

He kicked his shoes off, letting them fall with a soft thud onto the blue carpet of his bedroom floor. Sitting up, he took off his suit jacket and white dress shirt, wadding them up and throwing them in the general vicinity of his laundry basket. Lying back down he unbuckled his belt and took his slacks off, pushing them to the end of his bed.

Rolling onto his side, he closed his eyes and pictured Zellie's face as he leaned in to kiss her. He traced his lips with his index finger. He smiled, feeling dumb for calling what he and Zellie did just kissing. Again, he had overcome his fears and touched her, touched her the way he'd fantasized about, and it had been effortless, instinctual.

A sense of relief washed over him. The wondering was over. He let himself admit what he had been pushing down for a very long time. He loved Zellie and now he was certain she loved him too.

It had been two hours since my sixteenth birthday party had ended. Three hours since I had first kissed Avery. Four hours since I'd had the vision of him bleeding to death on the side of the road.

I'd spent the past twenty minutes trying to concentrate on the vision, that's what it was, about that I had no doubt. I wanted to figure out what it meant, but my mind kept wandering back to the kiss. I replayed my first kiss over and over in my head until the vision and my curiosity about it subsided. I was going to have to check with Claire, but I didn't think the whole "dry hump as first kiss" experience was normal. I could still sense the intensity of it vibrating in my bones.

Now, however, as I lay in bed listening to Melody snore, I needed to think about the vision without interrupting myself. Work through it.

First off, why did I have it? Was it my age? Was it because of Avery? Okay, if I was being truthful with myself, I wasn't completely shocked. My whole life I had known things about people. Like the game with Mom. I had always had a gut feeling about others lives, what they were sick with, if they were close to death. When I visited people after church with Mom on Sundays, I always saw if that person was going to get better or take a turn for the worse.

Second, why was the vision in the future? I now had a real picture in my mind to go along with my feelings, but Avery was not close to death in the present. We were both older. Avery's hair was gray at the temples and I was...pregnant. That's what was freaking me out the most. Still, I couldn't help but feel a small thrill run through me at the prospect that we would be together for longer than just a summer. We were going to have a baby together? Maybe it was all just a cruel cosmic joke? Maybe I wasn't freaking out enough about this. Shouldn't I be freaking out more about this?

Feelings, senses, I could keep to myself, I always had. But a possibly life-ending vision of the future? How was I going to keep that to myself? Who in the hell was I going to tell about it? My parents? They were sure to take me straight to the doctor. Maybe that was a good idea, I could probably use one.

I should start by telling Claire. She was the least likely to...well she would spaz out, but she might not think I was insane.

Avery was going to be the scariest to confess this to. Tomorrow, which was now today, after church at the lake, I would have to tell him then. Omitting, of course, the fact that I was in the vision and pregnant with his child. I was smart enough to know that informing him he was possibly my future husband and father of my child would probably not get me a second make-out session.

I took a deep breath, forcing my thoughts from my consciousness. I let myself slide into the feeling of Avery's arms around my waist, the clean sweet smell of his skin, the way he looked at me as he brought his face close to mine. Sweet, sweet dreams.

I awoke a short while later, Mom's hand on my forehead, a blank stare on her face.

The Avery vision flipped through my mind, but my eyes were all the way open. Unlike before, I could see the vision and what was right in front of me, which unfortunately was Melody clutching her creepy one-eared teddy bear. I looked up and studied Mom's face as the images of the smashed red pickup and Avery's wrecked body appeared. Her brow furrowed when I reached the part with me on my knees rocking back and forth, holding my stomach, covered in Avery's blood. Was I the only one seeing the vision? I didn't think so.

"Mom, what're you doing?" I jerked my head away from her touch.

"Oh, sorry honey," she whispered, coming to, "I didn't mean to scare you. I just thought that you looked a little feverish when you came home tonight. I wanted to make sure you were okay."

"I'm fine, Mom. Go back to bed." I rolled toward the wall, turning my back to her, trying to convince myself that she wasn't doing what I thought she'd been doing. Grace Wells, devoted mother, Pastor's wife, and bible group leader did not just read my mind.

"Goodnight, my sweet redheaded girl."

"Goodnight, Mom."

What in the frickity frack was going on? I pulled my blankets up over my head. So far, sixteen was turning out to be weird and more than I could deal with. Not to mention seriously screwing up my beauty sleep.

Chapter Five

I got up at five and jumped out of bed. I wanted to be the first person in the bathroom. Luxuriating in the hot shower, I smoothed a gigantic dollop of conditioner into my hair and let it linger while I meticulously shaved my legs. I scrubbed my arms, my stomach, the small of my back, and the tops of my feet with jasmine scented body wash. Forget tea rose perfume. This was the way to go.

I stepped from the shower and took two clean, but thin, towels from underneath the sink vanity. Securing one around my body, twisting the other around my hair. It was hard to breathe, the room was so steamy. I yanked open the small window above the toilet, letting the steam escape. I brushed my teeth, plucked my eyebrows, and cleaned my ears. Today, when Avery saw me I was going to look like perfection to him for once. All right, I admit it; I was in love, love, love! Something as momentous as that could cause a girl to go spastically hygienic.

At 6:30 Melody banged on the bathroom door. "Zellie! I have to pee so bad. Let me in."

I unlocked the door, struggling to turn the knob. I was almost done lotioning up.

Melody burst into the room, pushing me aside. She sat down on the toilet. "What are you doing in here? It smells like freaking Bath and Body Works exploded."

"Whatever," I trilled. She was not going to ruin my mood. There wasn't a thing in the whole universe that was going to bring me down. Okay, I was still practicing some major vision denial, but apart from that, nothing was going to bring me down today. Not when there was more severely hot making out to do!

I unwound my hair from the towel turban and combed through it with my fingers. Let the one hour blow dry commence.

Melody flushed the toilet. She turned on the shower, testing the water with her hand. I'm sure it was lukewarm. "Hey. You used up all the hot water."

I motioned that I couldn't hear her over the hair dryer. Nothing is gonna bring me down.

"Stupid Avery Adams," she hissed at me. "Did you hear that? I said your boyfriend is stoo-pid." Melody whipped off her nightshirt and hurried into the shower.

The goofiest grin in my repertoire spread across my face. She said my *boyfriend* was stupid. Yay to the...yay!

We Wells women splintered off to our various Sunday school classes. Mom led the adult Bible study, while Melody went to catechism class to prepare for her upcoming first communion. After your first communion you got to go to youth group, which was where I headed.

I tried to hold back a smile as I descended the stairs to the church basement.

Assistant Pastor Morris was walking around the long wooden table in the middle of the room placing Bibles on every other folding chair.

"Hey Zel, how was the birthday party?" he asked, handing me a Bible. I sat down at the end of the table.

I tried to play it coy. Pastor Morris was only like, twenty-three or something. He hadn't been an oblivious adult that long. "Oh, you know, as exciting as a party in a church basement can be."

"Wow, must have been a rager then." Pastor Morris winked at me and took his usual seat at the other end of the table.

All of the kids that had been at my party the night before began filing in and taking seats around the table. Avery and Jason walked into the room. Jason was kicking him on the back of his calves trying to make him fall down.

"Knock it off man," Avery said. He looked at me and smiled.

Of course, my face flushed hot pink.

There were three remaining empty chairs situated around the table, two on one side and one on the other. Avery made his way toward the two empty chairs, picking up a Bible off of one seat and sitting down. He put his hand on the seat of the other. He glanced at me.

Crap! How stupid could I be? Why hadn't I saved him a seat? I was already not being a good girlfriend. Now I was stuck at the end of the table. Pastor Morris was sure to tell Dad if he suspected anything.

Jason flicked Avery on the ear, went around to the other side of the table and sat in the last empty chair.

"Okay. Let's begin," Pastor Morris said. "Everyone join hands..."

Claire came running into the room, the wide neck of her black t-shirt hanging off her shoulder, exposing a lime green bra strap. "Sorry! My mom like, totally forgot where she put her car keys and didn't find them until like, five minutes ago. In the refrigerator of all places!"

She came to a halt next to the table. I could tell she had instantly comprehended my dilemma. "Zellie, be a dear and switch places with me, I am so not in the mood to share a Bible this morning."

"Sure!" I stood up lightning quick, almost knocking over my folding chair.

Claire crossed her eyes and made a fish face at me as we took our seats. Avery pushed the chair next to him back from the table so that I could sit down.

"Okay, now that everyone has arrived and is hopefully sitting in the chair that they want to be," Pastor Morris smirked, looking right at me, "let us all join hands and bow our heads in prayer."

I held Laura Weaver's hand with the fingertips of my right hand and gripped Avery's with my left.

"Heavenly father..." Pastor Morris began.

The smell of pine wafted up my nose.

"Zellie...I love...please."

I studied Avery's face. His jeans and long sleeve grey t-shirt were coated in blood. Bits of windshield were lodged in his forehead. A huge gash tore back the skin under his left eye.

"I could have prevented this. I could have stopped it." I heard my older self say as I rocked back and forth, holding onto my very pregnant stomach.

"Amen," the youth group said in unison.

"Amen," I added, realizing I'd spaced out again and missed the entire prayer.

After youth group Avery and I stayed in our chairs. Man, I was super duper colossally horrible at this whole girlfriend thing. Plan? What plan? I guess I thought we'd just sit here and everyone would leave and then we would get right on the making out. Ugh.

"I'll collect the Bibles, Pastor Morris. I know you need to get upstairs." Avery stood, Bible in hand, and began picking up the other Bibles scattered across the table.

"Thanks, Avery. Zellie can show you where they go. See you guys upstairs." Pastor Morris shot an amused look at both of us and then made his way upstairs to prepare for the service.

I got to my feet and wiped the palms of my hands down the front of my knee length floral printed skirt. "I'm glad you thought of something," I said, reaching out and picking up a few of the Bibles that were near me. "I guess I'm not too good under pressure."

"Yeah, it took me almost all of youth group to come up with this." He nodded to his stack of Bibles. "You usually put them away? I really don't know where they go."

"They go in my dad's office." I walked over to the door, looking back at him as I opened it.

Avery followed me into the room, kicking the door closed behind him with his foot. Hot. Can I get an Amen? H-O-T.

"Just set them here." I pointed behind me to the top of the filing cabinet I just happened to be standing in front of.

Avery leaned past me, his cheek skimming mine as he placed the Bibles on the filing cabinet. Pulling back, he gazed into my eyes. The spell of the night before had not been broken.

"You still want to meet at the lake this afternoon?" he said, licking his lips.

"Yes," I lifted my mouth to his and gave him a quick, sweet kiss, "how are you going to get there?"

He ducked his head. "Um, I have to ride my bike." Avery pulled back from me a bit.

"Good," I giggled, leaning in and kissing him again, "I do too."

He slid his hands down my forearms, grasping my hands in his. He smiled a crinkly-eyed smile at me. "Your skin is so soft. Just like I thought it would be."

"Thanks." I smiled back. If I had to get up at five in the morning for the rest of my life and loofah the bejeezus out of myself, it was worth it to hear him say that.

He drew me to him and kissed me once more, and then buried his face in my hair and took a big whiff. It was so good to know we were the same kind of perv.

Reluctantly, he pushed himself away from me. "I'll see you at three. Meet me by the picnic tables, okay?"

I looked at the big clock on the wall behind my dad's desk. Crud! We were seriously late for the church service. "Okay. I'll see you at three." I pushed him toward the door. "Hurry. Church has started already."

Chapter Six

It was 2:45. I was for sure going to be late to meet Avery. There was no way I was going to be able to make it home, change out of my church clothes, think of an excuse, and then ride my bike the three miles out to the lake.

Mom eased the minivan into the driveway. Both Melody and I shot out of the car, running through the house and into our room.

"Ick!" Melody said, collapsing on her bed. "I hate visiting sick people. Mom better not ever make me do that again."

"Yeah, well, she's being really weird today." I tore off my church clothes, slinging them over a hanger. "I'm supposed to meet Claire for a hike at the lake in like ten minutes and I'm going to be so late!"

"Bull," Melody said. She walked to her dresser, taking out a pair of shorts and pulled them on underneath her skirt.

"Bull what, Melody?" I didn't have the time to fight with or ask my sister for help. I kicked off my dressy white sandals.

"Bull you are meeting Claire at the lake. Everyone in church saw you and Avery coming in late to the service, including Mom." Melody pushed her skirt off over her shorts, letting it fall to the wood floor.

Mom opened our bedroom door and stuck her head in. "When you two are finished changing, come out to the back yard. I need help weeding the vegetable garden. Melody, pick up your skirt and hang it in the closet."

"But, Mom," I began, trying stay calm, "I promised Claire I would meet her out at the lake at three and now it's too late for me to call her and cancel."

"She has a cell phone doesn't she? Call her on that." She shook her head at me. "You know, you didn't ask for permission to go anywhere this afternoon. I don't appreciate that at all, young lady." Mom drew her head back into the hall and closed the bedroom door.

I couldn't help it; I threw one of the sandals after her. "Crap! What am I going to do now?"

"I guess you're going to help me and Mom weed the vegetable garden. You ruined my entire afternoon. I was supposed to be talking to Andy Cook on the phone since 1:30." Melody picked up the sandal. "But no, Mom thinks there's something going on and I get dragged along on the sick people visits to keep an eye on you." She threw the sandal back at me, just missing my head, and then flung the bedroom door open. "I can't wait to help you weed Mom! Zellie can't either! What a nice way to spend an afternoon!"

I sunk down to the floor and leaned back against my bed. I hoped Avery wouldn't be too mad at me. Worst girlfriend ever.

The fumes from the wood stain made Avery dizzy. He was pretty sure that he should be wearing some sort of breathing mask. It was just further proof that his father enjoyed torturing him. He slapped the paintbrush against the porch railing.

On a pissed off scale of 1-10 he figured Zellie was going to be about an 8. Their first kinda sorta date and instead of kissing her and talking to her and kissing her some more, here he was sweating his butt off, asphyxiating in the sun with his dad. Worst boyfriend ever.

"Make sure you get the stain in there real good. This isn't the time to be doing a half-assed job." His dad stood over him. "Okay...that's better. Good job."

Did his dad just give him a compliment? He was up to something.

The Adams men worked on staining the front porch for over an hour before his dad spoke. "Son, what were you doing with Zellie Wells during church today?"

Avery became intent on the railing he was working on. "Nothing, I don't know what you're talking about."

His dad set his paintbrush down, then took him by the shoulders, looking into his eyes. "You both came into the service late at the same time this morning. You have to be careful around her."

"Why?" Avery asked, backing out of his father's grip.

This time when his dad grabbed him by the shoulders, it was not so gently. "Listen, this is for your own good. Break things off with her now before you get in too deep."

"Dad, I like her, she likes me, that's it. I don't know why you're making such a big deal out of this." Avery resumed working on his railing.

"I don't want you to get hurt like...I need to keep you safe."

Avery was really confused, where was all of this coming from? Then he remembered how his Dad had behaved with Zellie's mom at the birthday party. Was he jealous? "We're not you and her mom, y'know." His dad blinked hard, taken aback. That *was* it. "Give me one reason why I shouldn't be with her, when you can't seem to be without Mrs. Wells." He tightened his grip on his paintbrush handle. "Don't think the entire town hasn't noticed how embarrassing you two are with each other."

"You will do as I say because I'm your father and I said so. That's reason enough." He let go of Avery's shoulders, looking at him with a glimmer of sadness in his eyes.

"Can we just finish staining the deck? I have a lot of homework to do." Avery turned away from his dad, more determined to be with Zellie than ever.

Sitting on his bedroom floor with his back against his bed, Avery pulled his shirt out from his chest and sniffed it. *Great*, he totally reeked of wood stain. He dialed Zellie's phone number, hoping she wasn't too mad at him for not showing up at the lake.

Pastor Paul answered the phone. "Hello?"

"Hi, uh, is Zellie there?"

"Who's calling?"

"It's Avery Adams, sir."

"Oh, Avery, hi, Zellie's mom has her doing hard labor out in the garden. Can I take a message?"

Wonderful, so it wasn't just him being imprisoned by his parents? What were they up to? "No, that's okay. I'll see her at school tomorrow. Thanks, um, bye."

"Bye."

Later that night he lay in bed fully clothed, listening for his parents. He'd heard his dad turn off the eleven o'clock news about a half hour before. They were sure to be asleep by now.

He crept from his bed, inching open his bedroom door and stepped out into the hallway. The wood floorboards creaked beneath him. This would have been so much easier if he could've fit through his bedroom window. He made his way to the garage, opened the side door and wheeled his bike out to the street before getting on it. He looked back at his house, everything was dark and still.

Riding his bike at this time of night was peaceful. All the houses were quiet, only a few had their TV's on, the light strobing though sheer curtains. The park by Zellie's house was empty, so much calmer when there weren't any kids in the sandboxes or on the swings. Avery noticed that they had reached the time of year when the city left the fountain flowing constantly. The night was hushed enough for him to hear the water cascading from the cherub's pitchers into the pool below.

He parked his bike at the end of the Wells' gravel driveway and made his way around the side of the house.

Walking down the length of it, he ran his hand along the siding to balance himself in case he tripped over something in the dark. Standing to the side of what he thought was Zellie's bedroom window; he tapped his fingers on the glass.

Someone was shaking me. "Zellie, wake up!" Melody whispered, "Avery's at the window."

"What?" I opened my eyes. I was clutching my belly. I'd been dreaming his vision.

"Avery's at the window, Zel. He wants to talk to you." Melody backed away and pointed outside. Avery waved at me.

I got up and opened the window. "Hey," I said, rubbing the sleep from my eyes. God, I must look horrible! Not to mention the fact that I was wearing my Minnie Mouse night shirt. The embarrassment, it seemed, would never end.

He stuck his head into the room and gave me a quick kiss on the mouth. "Hey, can you come with me somewhere?"

I looked at Melody sitting on her bed watching us like we were in a movie. "Right now?" I wanted nothing more than to go with him, but I was also afraid of getting grounded for the rest of my life.

Avery looked to Melody. "You're not going to say anything, are you Mel?"

"Not if Zellie gives me her allowance for the next two weeks, I won't." Melody spit on her hand and stuck it out to me.

I spit on my hand and shook Melody's. "Deal."

The excitement of what I was about to do was thrilling. I grabbed a pair of jeans from the closet and pulled them on under my night shirt. I debated for about two seconds whether I should put a bra on, but decided I couldn't be incognito enough to get it on with Avery standing right there. I was thankful for my nice little B-cups for once in my life. I slipped on my flip flops and then went to the window, trying to figure out the best way to climb through it without making too much noise.

Avery held the window all the way up while I stepped up onto my and Melody's desk. I slung my leg over the sill and ducked under the window pane. He put his arms around my waist, helping me out the rest of the way.

I let the window slide closed with a soft thud and mouthed "thanks" to Melody. Avery took my hand and led me around the side of the house down the driveway to where his bike was. “I’m sorry I didn’t meet you at the lake, my dad made me help him stain the deck.”

I smiled. It was a relief to know that I wasn’t the only one whose parents forced them to do chores. I think Claire would have to look the definition of chores up in the dictionary. “Yeah, well I was in weeding hell all afternoon and couldn’t get away either.” I put my arms around his waist, hugging him to me. “You’re here now and that’s all that matters. So, where are we going?”

Avery took my hands from around his waist. “Let’s walk over to the park across the street. I have some things I need to talk to you about.” He took hold of my hand and started walking.

This couldn’t be good. Had he decided that I was a dork after all? Had he realized that I was not worth his time? Was I too freakishly tall? Melody said guys didn’t like it when you were the same height as them. Did I not know how to gauge his feelings at all? No. I knew him. I already knew him. It had to be something besides me that was getting in the way of us.

We sat down on a bench underneath a street light. I could hear the water spilling from one level to the next in the fountain behind us. If what he was going to tell me was really bad I could always go drown myself in it. Let the cherubs take me down.

Avery turned to me, still holding my hand. “My dad doesn’t want me to start seeing you. He says that it’s for my own good, to keep me safe. Do you have any idea why he would say that?”

My hands began to tremble. Before I was kinda kidding about the fountain, but now maybe not. I’d been with Avery not even two whole days and now his dad was making him break up with me? And was he going to obey him and do it? "So your dad knows about us? What did you tell him?"

"I didn't tell him anything. He saw us both coming into church late and put two and two together I guess." Avery scooted closer, wrapping his arms around me to quiet the trembling that was taking over my body.

I searched his eyes, he was telling the truth. Of course he was. This was something our parents were doing to us. Avery still wanted to be with me. "My mom must know too, that's why she kept me from meeting you today. I honestly don't know why they would be trying to keep us apart."

He nodded. "You know they were engaged? Your mom and my dad?"

"Yeah, but for like a minute." Could that be why? That didn't seem fair at all and it was so long ago. I shook my head. "They were high school sweethearts. My mom said they broke up when she went away to school in St. Louis. They've been over for more than twenty years. You don't think that has anything to do with us, do you?"

"I don't know." Avery shrugged. "It just seems like the most logical explanation." His eyes grew wide and he loosened his grip on me just slightly. "Hey, you don't think we're, like, related or something?"

"No! Gross!" I slapped him on the chest. "There is no way that's what's going on. Yuck, I can't believe you said that!" Okay, it had crossed my mind for like a nanosecond, but I didn't want to have to change my firm "no" stance on incest, so I'd let it go. Too skeevy. I tried to pull away from him, but he just pulled me closer, laughing.

"Our moms were best friends too," he said. I've seen a picture of them with my dad and Jason's standing in front of your mom's old house before their prom. Maybe it has something to do with them not being friends anymore?"

"Maybe." I chewed my lower lip. This was something Claire and I had debated several times. "Do you know why they don't like each other? I mean, they were as close as me and Claire and I can't imagine us not being friends."

Avery looked up at the street light. "I think it might have something to do with my sister." His eyes met mine, his face somber now. "Did you know that? That I had an older sister? Her name was Erin. My family never talks about it."

"No, I've never heard any mention of her." That surprised me, not that I knew everything about Avery, but Rosedell was a pretty tight community, surely I would have heard about him having a sister? Something really bad must have happened-- Oh. The now familiar smell of pine began tickling my nose. "What happened to her?" I asked, not really needing to. Images of a baby girl, sprawled out on a hospital bed, tubes running up her nose and into her arms, flashed through my mind.

"She had leukemia." His eyes filled with tears and he looked away. "Actually, my parents partly had me because my bone marrow maybe would've helped her. She didn't...she died before I was old enough for it to be harvested."

This was the thing that Avery lived with. I was realizing his life wasn't as perfect as I'd always thought. Of course it wasn't. He could be beautiful, do well in school, be on every sports team, but he was born to save his sister and he thought he had failed at that.

Avery wiped his eyes with the back of his hand, facing me again. "Anyway, this one time after church? We were like, nine, I guess? I saw our moms having an argument over by the coat closet. Your mom kept trying to hug my mom, but she pushed her away. They were both crying. Then I heard my mom say Erin's name and your mom say she was sorry."

I turned in Avery's embrace, resting my head against his chest. "*I'm* sorry that happened to you. All of it. I don't know what my mom's deal was. Both of her parents died when she was our age and she can't...she probably wasn't there for your mom like she should've been."

Or she'd known what was going to happen and didn't say anything.

Mom always had the right answer in the game. It wasn't a parlor trick; she wasn't reading my mind, she was checking out my vision. She was like me, or I guess, I was like her. I felt a little relieved, knowing now that at least one person would believe my secret.

Guilt stepped on the back of relief's heels. Of course, Mom had royally screwed things up and broke her best friend's heart. I couldn't do that to Avery.

I had to get this over with and tell him. Holding back the vision from him, it was the wrong thing to do. "I have something to tell you. Kiss me first."

Avery took my face into his hands and pressed his mouth to mine, sliding his tongue between my lips. It was the most wonderful sensation. I tried to block out all the thoughts that were scratching at my brain and let myself go, relish the moment.

That worked for about no minutes. I kissed Avery more fervently and let the thoughts in. Could I live without him? I didn't want to, especially now that I knew what *this* was like. To have to stop touching him, I would go insane with need. So, then, how was I going to tell him about the vision? I had no way of proving any of it was real. Even if I was right about Mom, it wasn't like she was going to back me up and tell Avery the truth so I could keep making out with him.

I gave us each a second to catch our breath and then went back at him. I needed more time to think, which was not the easiest thing to do with a beautiful boy's beautiful mouth beautifully moving down...to review: Didn't want to live without him, needed him, wanted him, had to tell him, no help from anyone. Conclusion: He was going to think I was crazy and break up with me like his dad wanted him to.

I ran my hands through his hair, concentrating, just in case I needed to remember the feel of it should I become a boyfriendless loser again. It was silky soft, tickling the spaces between my fingers.

Ugh! Stupid Mom and her stupid hereditary visions. Was Melody going to get them too? Holy Christ on a cracker, the moral implications of Mel seeing the future were frightening. And Dad, I didn't have a clue if Dad knew anything.

I hadn't fully thought any of this out. What if there was more to this than I knew? I needed to talk to Mom first before I say anything to Avery. It couldn't hurt to learn from her mistakes. Right? That could also be the right thing to do.

My most dangerous and defeating thought finally wormed itself into my brain. The Avery vision wasn't going to happen for years and years. Tonight he was a hot fifteen-year-old boy with his arms around me in an embrace I never wanted to end. I had time to figure things out, time to develop a plan. At some point in the future I could be strong. Right now, I wanted to be kissed.

Avery ended the kiss, resting his forehead against mine, his eyes closed. "What did you want to tell me?"

I brushed my lips back and forth across his. I wasn't ready yet, I needed to find out more about the vision before I could give him up. "I wanted to tell you that no one, not my mom or your dad, can come between us. We're just going to have to be more careful when we're around each other."

I kissed him hard again, longing to feel my whole body electric. He responded, lying back on the bench and pulling me on top of him, grasping the back of my neck and pushing his tongue into my mouth.

Clearing my worries from my mind, I finally let myself savor the moment. I was losing control, my body taking over and I loved it. Without hesitation I sat up, straddling him, and yanked my nightshirt off.

Avery put his hands up to say stop, but then, as if he knew he was defeated, he reached out and brought me back down to him. I kissed his neck, my hands on his chest, pausing only to help push his shirt off over his head.

Amazingly I didn't hyperventilate; I was too busy feeling his bare skin against mine to even bother looking at him. I had wasted enough moments looking. He moved his hands down my back and grabbed my rear end.

For a second I considered stopping and telling him that I needed to go home, that I didn't know what I was doing out here half naked on a park bench. That I was sure I was going to hell for all of the things I wanted to do to him. But it felt so good.

The headlights from a passing car flashed over us.

"Whoa!" Avery clamped his arms around me. We lay there nose to nose, looking at each other.

I totally got the giggles. "Are you trying to shield me?"

He grinned. "Um, don't know if you've noticed, but you don't have a shirt on."

I pulled away and slapped him on the chest. “You don’t either!”

He grabbed my wrist, pulling me down. He kissed me, getting back into it, then he stopped abruptly and in a strained voice said, “We gotta go home Zel, or we’re liable to get ourselves arrested for public indecency.”

I got up, stumbling a little, and picked my nightshirt up off the ground, “I can’t believe I’m going to say this,” I said as I shook the dust from my shirt and put it on, “but it was just about to get a lot more indecent out here.”

Avery stood, putting his shirt on and pulling it down in front. “Yeah, we gotta go home right now.”

The next morning I lay in bed, getting my nerve up. I heard Mom shuffle down the hallway and go into the kitchen. Melody and Dad were still asleep. Now was my chance. I quietly got up and checked myself out in the mirror. I didn’t see any signs of hickies or puffy lips. Crud! My nightshirt was on inside out. That would not have been good. I turned it right side out. Okay. I was ready.

Mom was making coffee. I went to the fridge and got out the orange juice. “Morning,” I said.

She yawned, covering her mouth with her hand. “Morning, Zel. How’d you sleep?”

I poured a small glass of juice. “Pretty good. Although, y’know, I keep having this crazy dream about how Avery Adams is going to die.” Might as well get down to it. “Um, it takes place in the future...and I’m also pregnant in it.” I gulped down the juice and poured another glass.

Mom put her hands out, bracing herself against the countertop. She exhaled and then took a deep breath in.

I concentrated on the Last Supper magnet holding the church newsletter to the fridge. "Don't worry though," I assured her, "I think we're married. So, um, the baby..." I put the orange juice back in the fridge and turned to look at her. "Please say something."

Instead of saying anything, she went down the hall to her bedroom and came back into the kitchen holding some folded up pieces of green paper. She handed them to me. "Everything I know about this is in that letter. Quick, read it before your dad and Melody wake up."

I sat down at the kitchen table. Mom hovered over my shoulder, reading the letter with me.

Dear Gracie,

I want to start by telling you that I'm sorry honey and I hope you can someday forgive me for what I have done.

There are many things that you do not know about me. Things that have led me to make the decision to take my own life.

Everything I'm about to tell you is true. All that I ask is that you read this letter and keep it in the back of your mind.

Growing up, I always knew that I was different. I could sense things. Sometimes silly things, like knowing what all of my Christmas presents were even though they were wrapped. Sometimes horrible things like knowing the exact night that our neighbors, the Bucks, house would burn to the ground.

I kept my feelings to myself. Many times I thought that maybe I was crazy.

After the Bucks' house burned (I was thirteen at the time) and the whole family perished in the fire, the guilt that I could have warned them overtook me.

I vowed from that point on to trust my feelings and do whatever I could to stop any other tragedies from occurring.

One afternoon I sat on the banks of the lake for several hours. I had an overwhelming feeling that a small child was going to drown. Sure enough, around four o'clock as my eyes scanned the lake, I saw Alexander Bitman go under the water and not come back up. I alerted the lifeguard on duty, who rescued Alexander. I never doubted my abilities again.

This next part of my story you have heard bits and pieces of over the years, but this is the whole truth.

In July, the summer after I graduated from Rosedell High, I went to a party at my friend Edna's house. Edna's boyfriend Ron brought your dad to the party. He was a new face in town, a young lawyer from Portland that Ron had convinced to move to Rosedell and open up a law practice with him.

I was immediately drawn to your father. He was such a smart handsome man. That night after spending just a few hours talking to him, I knew that I would fall in love with him and marry him. For me Gracie, it was not just love at first sight like your father and I always joked about. I felt the connection between us. I knew that he was the one I was meant to be with.

About a month after we met, your dad and I were standing outside of Wechsler's Drugstore. As he leaned in to kiss me I was overwhelmed by the smell of rain. Then I had a vision of his death. I saw it as plain as day. He was older and lying in the grass next to a red rose bush in front of a yellow house. He clutched his chest with his left hand, a gold wedding band on his ring finger. I came running from the house, older too, the screen door slamming behind me.

Although the visions were new to me, I dealt with them the same way that I did with my other abilities. I never told your father that I had seen his death. I thought that I could change the course of the future by altering little things. I made sure that we never lived in a yellow house. I never planted red rose bushes. I even acted like I thought screen doors were the most hideous things on earth! Our wedding bands are silver. But, you know the end of this story. He died anyway, lying in the front yard clutching his chest. There was nothing about that part of the vision that I could change.

The strange thing was, after I had that first vision of your father, I started having visions of things that happened to other people. I was able to save them without fail, to the point that, as you know, people grew suspicious of why I was always around when accidents were narrowly averted. I know that this embarrassed you, that folks in town thought I was a little crazy or maybe bad luck. I'm sorry for that too, Gracie, but it feels good to finally let you know that I was saving their lives.

Why then couldn't I save your father's life? It is a question that has plagued me these two months since his death. After much contemplation I have come to some conclusions:

1. I think that the true love of your father triggered the visions. I had never felt for another man what I did for him.

2. Because I married him I did not alter the future enough to prevent him from dying in the manner he did in the vision.

3. Every night since I first had the vision of your father's death I dreamt of it and it never changed. Then the night before he died, I didn't have the dream at all. I thought that was a good thing. I had stopped having the vision when I touched him many years before. However, it was a sign I ignored. I let my guard down.

Honey, I'm telling you these things not only because I needed to come clean about who I am, to give you some insight as to why I would have such an immense sense of guilt that I would end my own life, but because I fear that you may have inherited my abilities.

As a child I observed that you were very cautious and protective of others and extremely hard to surprise! I don't know if I was seeing something that I wanted to see. We never talked about it and I never had visions or senses about you. I think I thought maybe your own abilities would take care of you.

Gracie, if you do have abilities similar to mine, please learn from my mistakes. Save yourself a lifetime of trouble and heartache. I'm sorry that I don't have more knowledge about this to share with you. I don't know where the visions came from, perhaps this is a mystery you can solve for the both of us.

The only other person I have told about any of this is your aunt Hazel. She has always been a wonderful sister to me and I know she will be a wonderful guardian for you. She does not have the senses or the visions, but she knows everything that I have just told you. Go to her for anything you need, you can trust her.

Take care my sweet red headed girl.

Love Always,

MOM

"Is this why you didn't marry Avery's dad?"

She nodded.

Tears were rushing to the surface. This was a hundred times worse than I thought it would be. I was just about to freak the freak out.

There was *nothing* I could do. Avery was really going to die the way I'd seen it. Forget marrying him or having a baby with him. We could never even be together. Oh God. My heart sank. I loved him so much already. How was I going to stand being near him knowing he couldn't be mine? Loving me was literally going to kill him. I blinked away my tears. Please don't let this be happening. I read through the three rules in the letter one more time and gave it back to Mom.

She wrapped her arms around me, hugging me. I could hardly feel it. She kissed the top of my head. That was it? That was the comforting? The explanation? A frickin' letter and a hug and a kiss and "Sorry Zel, I had to ruin my true love, so you have to ruin yours."

I stared at the cuckoo clock on the wall. It was going to go off soon.

"You knew about Erin?" I asked, "That she was going to die and you didn't tell Mrs. Adams? That's why she doesn't like you?"

"Yes." Mom said into my hair. "Mike called me one night when I was in St. Louis and told me that Becky was pregnant, that they were getting married. I had the vision then." She kissed my head again. "I saw Avery too...well that there would be an Avery. I was glad for that." She smiled.

"You weren't mad? At Mrs. Adams, I mean? She was your best friend and she stole your true love."

She shook her head. "I wasn't mad. It was the best thing that could've happened, the two people that I loved the most in the world taking care of each other."

"But they're not taking care of each other, they're miserable."

"That is not my fault, although it's yet another thing Becky blames me for."

If I was Mrs. Adams, I would blame her too. No one is that selfless. "Why did you move back here then?"

She carried on with the story. "After Erin was diagnosed, Mike called again. He'd found a job for your dad at Trinity Lutheran and wanted us to move back here." She studied my face. I gave her nothing.

"I knew they were going to need me, I wanted to be there for both of them, so we moved. But, I waited a while, too long, to tell Becky about the vision and by that point she thought I'd withheld it to get back at her for being with Mike. She's not going to forgive me." Mom let go of me and sat down at the table.

"You thought telling her was the right thing to do?" I asked.

She shrugged her shoulders. "Well, in retrospect, no. I shouldn't have told anyone anything. I should have stayed in Missouri and never moved back here. But that's not what I did and so I deal with what is the best way I know how."

"And you've never told Dad?" I looked at the clock again. Three minutes to cuckoo.

Mom sighed. "No. Apart from my lack of judgment in telling Becky, no one knows except for Mike and Aunt Hazel."

She turned the letter in her hands, rubbing it between her fingers. "Do you understand the rules? It's best to stop this thing with Avery before you get in over your head. Believe me." She brushed my hair back from my face. "I know what happens in the vision isn't actually going to happen for a long time, but you can't be too careful."

Two minutes. "Do you still dream about Mr. Adams?"

"Every night. Thank God." Mom grabbed my hand, transferring her vision of Mr. Adams to me.

I could see everything, like her thoughts were my own. It was awful. Mr. Adams sitting behind a desk, fear in his eyes, the muddled reflection of a woman aiming a gun at him, the bullet wound to his face, Mom standing behind him screaming her head off, the sheer heartbreak of it all. Tears spilled from my eyes. "And you got this vision right away? When you and Mr. Adams started...dating?"

She shook her head. "No. It took three years." Tears started running down her face too. She blinked them back. "I thought I wasn't going to have visions. I got the first one right after he proposed marriage to me. That's why it was particularly painful to let him go. Why I had to get out of Rosedell." She balled her fists, digging her nails into her palms.

"I know better than anyone Zel, what it feels like, how much you must already love him, but please, please save Avery's life. It hasn't been easy for me and it won't be for you, but the sacrifice is worth it."

Dad strolled down the hall singing. He knocked twice on my bedroom door on his way to the kitchen. "Morning has bro-ken, like the first more-ha-horn-nin."

"Cuck-coo! Cuck-coo!"

I got up from the table in a daze, Mom grabbed my wrist, "You will find someone else to be happy with."

I pulled from her, mumbling, "I have to get ready for school." I rubbed the tears from my eyes and attempted to smile at Dad.

"Everything okay in here ladies?" he said. He stood before the open refrigerator, examining its contents.

Mom slipped her mother's letter into her robe pocket and went back to making coffee. "Girl stuff, I've got it under control."

"Ah." Dad loaded up his arms with a carton of eggs, a bag of cheddar cheese, some deli ham, and some chives. He turned to me. "Omelet?"

"Yes, please," I said. With a side of denial.

Chapter Seven

In the weeks since Avery appeared at my window, things between us had become very serious. He'd visited me late at night a few more times, resulting in more park bench maneuvers. But we had to be careful, I knew after my conversation with Mom that getting caught was not an option.

The only other time that we could be alone together was at school and we met every day during lunch under the bleachers by the football field. It was probably the most educational part of our school day. We tried, we really did, to spend a few minutes talking about something, school, parents, friends, but most of our lunch hours were taken up by making out. I found it very hard to be around Avery and not touch him in some way.

To keep his dad and my mom from suspecting anything was still going on with us, we didn't sit next to each other at youth group or arrive late to the church service. It took all the self control I could muster not to look at Avery throughout the entire sermon. And now, school was ending in a few days and so would our daily meetings. Good thing I'd finally had enough foresight to come up with a plan.

Rosedell got oppressively hot in June and stayed that way until early October. It made being outside pretty miserable. I didn't know how Avery could stand to play soccer in this heat. The upside was that even pastor's daughters could get away with wearing less clothing. Okay, I was maybe, despite the inevitable agony that lay before me, enjoying being a mildly slutty girl. After sixteen years of turtlenecks and hand-me-down floral print dresses, it was freeing to flash a bit of skin.

I showed up under the bleachers wearing a pair of cut off jean shorts and a light blue tank top, my long red hair piled up on top of my head, exposing the back of my neck. I was starting to know exactly what got Avery's motor running.

I sat down next to him on one of the two milk crates we'd pushed together for a place to sit. He kissed me first thing.

I kissed him back, taking one of his hands and slipping it up under my tank top.

Avery pulled himself out of the kiss, letting his hand slide down my side and rest on my hip. "Well, hello to you too."

I laughed. "Hey man, we haven't got much time." I moved his hand back up my shirt.

Avery withdrew his hand in mock surprise. "Who are you and what have you done with my innocent little girlfriend?"

I leaned back on the palms of my hands and stretched my legs out. "Little?" I asked, eyeing all five feet eleven inches of myself up and down. "Innocent?" I reached over and pulled him to me, kissing him hard on the mouth.

Avery took the initiative this time, skimming his hand under my shirt.

The electricity was always there now, crackling between us and I was addicted to it. He was too, only he didn't know why. It wasn't only love, it couldn't be. This affliction that I had, the visions, it had caused me to need the bond between us. I craved him so much, I couldn't even feel guilty about it.

I could not force myself tell him about the visions. Severing our bond would break his heart and mine. The idea of the two of us ending up like our parents, waving to each other through office windows, living for idle chit-chat on Sunday morning, was devastating.

Avery drew his head back and looked into my eyes. “What’re we going to do when school’s out? I don’t know if I can stand not seeing you every day.”

I sat up. I’ll admit I was a little bit excited about my plan. “I’m glad you asked. I’ve been thinking. Why don’t we take turns sneaking out of our houses a couple of nights a week? On Fridays I can spend the night at Claire’s and I’ve lined up a Saturday night babysitting job with the Hitzerts. They’re always out until like, midnight, and they just have one little baby that sleeps most of the time.

“That gives us two weekend nights and probably, just to be safe and not arouse too much suspicion, three week nights. I was thinking Monday, Tuesday, and Wednesday. We’ll take Thursdays off to hang out with friends, but you can always call me on Claire’s cell. Sound good?”

Avery gawked at me, visibly impressed.

“What?” I grinned and punched him on the arm.

He grabbed my hand. “You made a plan.”

Of course I blushed. “Yes, I made a plan.”

He pulled me to him, planting soft kisses on my nose and eyelids. “I’ll take Mondays and Wednesdays.”

Avery rode his bike towards his dad’s office, bummed, because soon his after school job was going to turn into full time summer employment. If it wasn’t for Zellie, he would be spending yet another summer vacation envying all of his friend's plans for camping and road trips to the coast and Portland like he always did. At least now if his days had to suck, his nights looked promising.

He rounded the corner and turned onto Cascade Ave. Up ahead, a small crowd had gathered in front of the insurance agency. Something wasn't right. Avery pedaled faster, his heart racing. What the hell was going on?

Juanita, his mom's boss at the hair salon, noticed him and waved him over. Several people turned to look at who she was waving at. That's when he noticed his mom's Camry parked halfway on the street and halfway on the curb. His gaze shifted from the car to his mom, still dressed in her smock, the metal hair clips attached to it glinting in the sun. She looked like she was about to kick in the office door.

"Mom! Mom!" he called to her. He jumped from his bike, rushing to her side. "What's the matter?"

"Avery...I can't get in. Do you know where your father is?" She burst into tears, her face distorted with pain and red hot anger.

"No, I don't know where he is, he should be here. Listen, Mom, what's wrong? Stop freaking out for a second and talk to me." Avery attempted to wipe his mother's eyes with the end of his t-shirt.

She backed away from him and collapsed to the ground, huddling up against the office door. "Not until you get all of these people out of here." She glared at the bystanders. "Nothing to see here folks! Just a woman having a nervous breakdown."

Most of the people got the message and walked away. Juanita gave Avery a questioning look.

"We're fine," he said, "thanks. I've got it under control."

"You let me know if you need anything, sugar." Juanita shooed the remaining gawkers away, got into her car and drove off.

Avery looked down at his mom. "Okay, everyone's gone, now tell me what going on?"

"Look in the front seat." She pointed to the haphazardly parked car, her hand shaking. "Your father's divorcing me and taking you away from me. He says I'm crazy, that I'm unfit. I'm not unfit, am I honey?"

"What? What are you talking about?" Avery went to the car and picked up the papers that were strewn all over the front seat. Some of them were wet with alcohol. Noticing the flask on the floor, he quickly tossed it back into the glove compartment.

He sat down on the sidewalk next to his mom, rearranging the papers and trying to make sense of what the pages said. After reading for a few moments he turned to her. "Why would he do this? Did you stop taking your medicine again?"

She looked away from him. "You know how that stuff makes me feel, Av. I don't feel like myself. I don't feel anything."

He put his arm around her shoulders. "Mom, you promised me. Dad said he would leave if you did this again."

She grabbed his hand and kissed the top of it. "You're not going to leave me, are you honey? I don't care if he goes, but you have to stay. Promise me you won't go."

Avery took his arm from around his mother and got to his feet. "Come on. Let's go home and wait for him. You can take your medicine and everything's going to be okay. I'm not going anywhere."

She took his hand, letting him pull her up. “Okay, put your bike in the back. We’ll go home.” She walked to the car and popped the trunk before she slumped into the driver’s seat.

Avery heaved his bike into the car and then stowed the divorce papers in his backpack. He walked around to the driver’s side, took his mom’s hand and helped her out of the car and around into the passenger side seat. Taking over the driver’s seat, he started the car. It wasn’t that far to the house and his mother was in no shape to drive.

The door from the kitchen to the garage opened and Avery’s dad glared at him, no doubt surprised to see his son driving the car. “What the hell are you doing?” he said, “You’re not allowed to drive yet.”

Avery got out of the car, slinging his backpack on, ignoring him. He went around to the passenger side door and helped his mom from the car. Walking with his arm around her waist, the two of them went into the house, nudging his dad aside.

He led his mother to her bedroom, took off her shoes and work smock, propped her up in bed and then went into the bathroom and shook a Zoloft and a Xanax from their prescription bottles. He filled a glass with water and waited while his mother took the pills. There was probably no use in making her take her meds now, but it was all he could think of to do. He pulled the covers up over her shoulders. “Don’t worry Mom, I’ll take care of this.” *Somehow.*

His dad stood in the bedroom doorway watching, shaking his head.

Avery walked past him into the hall, motioning for him to shut the bedroom door.

Sitting down at the dining room table, he took his backpack off and ripped the largest compartment open. He threw the rumpled manila envelope containing the divorce papers at his dad. "What the hell are *you* doing?"

"I didn't know she was off her meds, Son. I didn't think she would take it like this. I figured she might even be relieved." His dad picked up the scattered papers from the floor and sat down at the table.

Avery snorted. "Bull! You said she was crazy! You said she was unfit. She's not the unfit parent, you are. You just drop a bomb like this on both of us and then... where the hell were you this afternoon?" He had a good idea. Despite his dad's recent shower, Avery could still smell Mrs. Wells distinctive rose perfume that she always wore all over him. He felt sick to his stomach, he had to get out of here. Looking at his dad, he felt his hands clench into fists. He'd never wanted to hit someone so much in his entire life. He stood, turning to flee the room.

His dad grabbed his arm. "Avery. Your mom and I have not been happy for a long time. You know that. She obviously needs some help and I will help her. But I cannot stay married to her. You and I have got to get out of here. This town is suffocating the both of us."

He jerked his arm from his father's grip. "What are you talking about? I'm happy. I'm happier than I've ever been and now you're going to take me away from here, from my home?"

"It's for the best. You'll see. I'm doing this for you. It's not safe here for you anymore."

Avery picked up his backpack and flung it at his father's head. "Stop. Just stop with all of this cryptic crap and tell me why! What's not safe? Mom? Mom's not going to hurt me." His Dad shook his head. "What? Is it Zellie then? You think she's going to do something to me? Zellie *loves* me, Dad. Just who the hell am I not safe around? Because as far as I can tell you're the only one threatening me!" He ran to his room, slamming the door with such force that the house shook.

After a moment he heard the front door close. Avery looked out his bedroom window and saw his dad sling his overnight bag into the cab of his truck. *Good. He wants to leave so bad, he can leave by himself.*

Relieved that his dad was gone, he walked down the hall and checked on his mom to see how she was doing. Zonked out, that's how she was. Jesus, had she even heard them fighting? She must have had way more to drink than he thought. He tiptoed over to her bedside and put a finger under her nose. Still breathing. What was he doing? His mom was fine, she'd sleep it off like she had many times before.

The person he should be worrying about was himself. Zellie. He needed to see Zellie now and there was only one way he could do that on a school night.

Claire's phone rang seven times before she answered it.

"You rang?"

Oops, he'd made a mistake. Whoever he was talking to sounded like they were on a walkie-talkie in an underwater cave. Definitely not Claire's scene. He checked the number he'd dialed on the phone. It was her number. "Claire?"

"Yes?"

"It's Avery." He paused. "You sound funny."

"That's because I'm under my bed," she said, like that explained everything.

"Oh." He was eternally confused by her.

"Is there something I can help you with, Mr. Adams?"

"Yes. Are your parents out of the house?"

"Naturally."

"Good." He let out the breath he'd been half holding. Everything was going to be okay. "Do you think you can get Zellie to come over? I need to see her."

"I suppose I could, but why don't you just wait a few hours and then sneak over to her house? I hear that you've been oh-so-romantically showing up at her window in the middle of the night, Romeo," Claire teased.

"I need to see her now. I wouldn't ask if it wasn't important," Avery pleaded.

"Got it," she said, all trace of teasing gone from her voice, "Give me half an hour."

"Thanks. You're a good friend." Avery let his breath out the rest of the way.

"Yeah, yeah, I'm extremely familiar with the "F" word. See you in a few."

The phone rang in the kitchen. Melody and I both jumped up from the dinner table to answer it. She got to it first.

"Hello, Wells residence, Melody speaking."

I could hear Claire's voice. I tried to grab the phone away, but Mel hunched over it holding it to her chest.

"And who may I ask is calling?" she said with faux politeness.

Claire went off, yelling loud enough I could almost make out what she was saying. Something about Avery? I pinched the back of Melody's arm as hard as I could.

"Ow!" She yanked her arm away from me. "I'm sorry, we've just sat down to dinner. May I take a message?"

"Melody!" I yelled, exasperated.

"Fine!" She shoved the phone at me. "It's Claire."

"Yes. I know." I stared her down until she left the room. "Hey. What's up?"

"Hey. Listen, Avery just called me. He needs to see you and wanted me to get you over to my house somehow."

"Really?" I lowered my voice. "You know my parents won't let me go out on a school night." I paused. "Are you under your bed again?"

"Yes," Claire sighed. "Tell them that my dog died and I need some comforting,"

"You don't have a dog."

"They don't know that, do they?"

"No. I suppose not. Hold on, let me ask them."

I put the phone down and went into the dining room. Mom and Dad were fussing over the red welt I'd made on Melody's arm. Whoops. I cleared my throat to get their attention and slipped into my best good girl voice. "Um, may I please go over to Claire's house for a little bit this evening? Her dog died and she's really sad about it."

Mom looked at me weird. With sadness? Anger? I couldn't tell. "Are her parents home?"

I ran back to the phone. "They wanna know if your parents are home."

"Tell them that they went out to pick up some Chinese food and will call them as soon as they get home."

"Good one." I set the phone down, lied to my parents about Chinese food and then returned quickly. "Okay. I'll be over when we're finished with dinner. Dad's going to drop me off. He says he's sorry about your dog."

"Yes, um, tell him thanks and that Rover will be missed. Okay, I'll make sure there are no signs of Avery. Over and out."

"Thanks, Claire."

"Whatever girl, just get over here, that boy needs you."

While I waited for Dad to finish off his eighteenth helping of scalloped potatoes, I searched for something cute to wear. Only problem? Nothing cute to wear. My like, two semi-flattering tank tops weren't in my dresser or the laundry basket. Maybe Mom knew. She'd gone to lie down right after Claire called and I probably should leave her alone, but it was a cuteness emergency.

I knocked softly on my parents' bedroom door, peeking around it. "Can I come in?"

"Sure honey, come in." Mom sat up on the bed and wiped her eyes. Had she been crying?

I stuck my head into the room. "Do you know where my yellow tank top is, the one with the little daisies on the straps?"

"I think it's in the dryer, Zel, I washed it yesterday." She rubbed her face.

"Cool, thanks." I started to shut the door.

"Tell Claire I'm sorry about her dog. Love you, honey."

"Love you, too." I closed the door. Avery needed to see me and Mom was hiding out in her bedroom crying? Not a good sign.

Chapter Eight

I climbed into the minivan, anxious to get to Claire's house. Thank God the drive only took ten minutes.

"Sorry I took so long eating dinner. You know how I love those scalloped potatoes that come in the box. They must have an addictive drug in them or something," Dad said, a devilish grin on his face.

"That's fine," I turned to look out the window. Whatever, Dad! Let's get a move on. Something was up with Avery and it was killing me not to be there with him. "I just hope Claire isn't distraught. She really loved that dog."

"What was its name again?" He slowed the minivan down, having chosen to drive through the only school zone in town.

"Uh, Rover." Crud. I was such a sucktastic liar when it came to him.

"Interesting. Y'know, Zellie, you're a really bad liar."

I turned to him, my face burning red. I'd been found out. Oh God, where was he taking me? Surely not to Claire's? No. He was taking me to a nunnery! Wait, we were Lutheran. What was the equivalent? Was there an equivalent? Ugh. Be cool, just be cool. "What? What are you talking about?"

Dad chuckled. "I know Claire doesn't have a dog, her mother has horrible allergies to all sorts of things. Give me a little credit. It's my business to know about my congregation."

"Then why are you letting me go to Claire's house?" We were going to her house right? Please, God, I swear I will dial down the making out, just please let us be really going to Claire's.

"Well, I'd rather have you hanging out with Avery at her house than sneaking out with him in the middle of the night."

I sank down in my seat, shocked. "You know about that?"

Dad steered the minivan over to the side of the road and put it in park. I put my hand on the door handle in case I had to make a quick getaway.

He turned to me. "A long time ago before I became a pastor, I was a fifteen-year-old boy. I snuck out of my house to go see Roselyn Finn at least three times a week one summer. My father, at the end of that summer, let me know that he knew what I was doing too."

I was starting to see his angle. "And I suppose you were grounded until you met Mom?"

He shook his head. "Zellie, since the beginning of time, teenagers have been sneaking out and inventing reasons to spend the night at their friends' houses. If we had a second story on the house I have absolutely no doubt that Avery Adams would be climbing up trees or hiding a ladder in the bushes so that he could scale up it and appear at your window. I have decided not to fight against the inevitability that you will act like a teenager."

I straightened up a little in my seat. Dad was being really cool. That must mean... "Does Mom know?"

"No, she doesn't know for now. I thought we could keep this between the two of us and not worry her. Your mom was a bit of a wild child when she was your age. I think she's afraid that you're going to pay her back, karmically speaking. But your mom lost both of her parents at fifteen. She had a lot of anger and sadness to get out of her system. I think you're more like me, more interested in the romance of sneaking out of the house than the thrill or the defiance of it. Your conscience will prevail. Now with Melody..." He gave me a wink.

"Wow, Dad, that's really cool of you." I blushed. I was seven kinds of guilty. If he only knew.

"Yes. I know." He put the car in drive and pulled away from the curb, checking his rearview mirror for oncoming traffic. "That being said, I will be back at eleven to pick you up. It is a weeknight after all and you have school in the morning. Also, I'm fairly certain that Claire's parents aren't home. Please have them give me a call when they do get back. See how this is gonna work, Zel? I give a little, you give a little."

"Thanks, Dad."

"No problem, sweetheart."

Dad came to a stop in front of Claire's house. "Here we are, Madame. See you at eleven."

I leaned over to give him a hug goodbye. As I wrapped my arms around his neck I got a sickening feeling in my gut. He smelled of pine.

A vision flashed through my head. I saw him wrestling with a woman, her hair covering her face. She had a gun in her hand. Dad was trying to shake the gun from the woman's hand, banging her arm against the side of a black leather couch. There was screaming, but I couldn't make out the voices or the woman's face. I could see Dad's hand slip from the woman's arm. Then she regained her grip on the gun and aimed it at his face and shot.

"Okay, honey, I get it, you love me. I'll see you in a few hours."

I snapped back into the present. I was almost strangling him in my embrace. I let go of him and looked into his eyes. He smiled at me. "I'll see you soon, Dad. Thanks for driving me and everything." I opened the minivan door and hopped out. As I walked up Claire's driveway, he honked the horn at me and waved. I turned and waved back.

Dazed, I rang the doorbell instead of walking into the house like I normally would.

Claire answered the door. "Oh crap, not you too."

"Me too, what?" I said as I entered the house.

"Something bad happened to you too, you don't look so good." Claire shut the front door behind us.

"I'm fine, really. Where's Avery?" I started off down the hall towards the kitchen.

"He's--" Claire started to say.

"Zel, I'm up here," Avery called from the top of the stairs.

I backtracked and ran up the stairs, Claire following behind me.

At first Avery looked relieved to see me, but then his expression changed to worry. I went right for him, throwing my arms around his neck and kissing him.

He squeezed me tightly "Are you okay?"

I pulled away from him and looked over my shoulder at Claire. "What's up with you guys? I'm fine." There wasn't anything I could do about anything right now. I didn't know what I would do if I could. We had to get Avery's problem figured out first anyhow. I studied his face. "Are you okay?"

"No, I'm not." He took my arms from around his neck and led me into Claire's room. He sat down on the floor with his back against the bed, pulling me down next to him. Claire stood in the doorway.

"Do you want me to leave you guys alone? I can go watch TV downstairs or something."

"Yeah," Avery said, "maybe you'd better. Thanks again."

"Okay, you two, holler if you need anything." She shut her bedroom door.

Avery turned to me and took my hands in his. "Things are bad. My dad served my mom with divorce papers today."

I squeezed his hand tighter. "What happened? Why?"

He looked down. "I should have told you this. I've been meaning to, but it's embarrassing and really, I don't know...hard to admit? My mom's sick and she um, kind of goes crazy when she doesn't take her medicine."

I wrapped my arms around him, hugging him to me. Well that just plain sucked for everyone. "Your poor mom, what's going on?"

He laid his head in my lap. I stroked his hair while he told me about it. "Once or twice a year she does this. The last time was really bad. She, um, cut my dad's head off in every picture that we had of him and locked herself in the bathroom for a whole day. She wouldn't talk to anyone, she just kept passing me notes under the door that didn't make any sense at all."

"Oh, Avery, I'm so sorry. That's horrible." I had to lean away from him a little. The smell of pine was itching its way into my nose.

"Anyway, after the last time, Dad threatened to have her committed and divorce her if she ever stopped taking her medicine again. I guess she did. I mean, I know she did so..." He looked up into my eyes like he was checking to make sure I wasn't about to run from him and all of his crazy mom baggage. As if. I pulled it together and gave him a comforting smile.

He started again. "Well, there's more. When I went to my dad's office after school today, she was standing outside freaking out. I took her home and gave her medicine and everything but the divorce papers...my dad said she's crazy and he's suing for sole custody of me. He's taking me away, Zellie. He's making me leave with him. I don't know what to do."

I held his face in my hands, forcing him to look at me. "Listen, we're going to figure this out. Let's call my dad and see if he can help us. Y'know maybe he'll let you stay with us while your mom gets herself together."

He sat up. "Your dad is not going to let his daughter's boyfriend that he doesn't even know about crash on the couch. That is not going to work."

The bedroom door opened a crack and Claire spoke from out in the hall. "You can stay here, I'm sure my parents wouldn't even notice."

"Thanks for the privacy Claire!" I said a little too harshly. "Look, my dad knows about us, he will help you, I promise."

"Since when does your dad know about us?" Avery said, taken aback.

"He just told me on the way over here. I know it seems like a long shot, but he could help your mom too, he could--"

My eyes snapped shut, automatically blocking out Claire's room and Avery, forcing me to focus on the scene playing out in my mind.

I watched as Mrs. Adams parked her car in the lot behind Adams Insurance and turned off the ignition. She popped the trunk, got out of the car and walked around to the back of it. Lifting the lid part way, she eased a black duffel bag from the inside, scanning the street to see if anyone was looking at her. Downtown was deserted.

She slung the duffel over her shoulder and walked to the back entrance of the building. She tried the knob. The door was locked. Looking around again, she dropped the bag to the ground and unzipped it. She pulled out a crow bar. Wedging it in between the door jamb and the lock, she anchored it back. The metal of the door jamb bent and the lock popped open. She slid the bag into the hallway and went inside, closing the door behind her. She put the crowbar back in the bag and pulled out a gun.

Tiptoeing down the short hall, she came to two saloon doors and looked over the top of them. Mr. Adams was asleep on the couch.

She crept up to him, aimed the gun at his forehead and cocked it. "Get up."

Mr. Adams eyes shot open and focused on the gun aimed between them. "Becky?"

She reached down and grabbed her husband by his shirt collar. "I said get up!"

He put his hands up in front of him and stood. "Becky, what are you doing? Let's talk about this. We can talk about this. I didn't know you were off your meds. That was a definite bad on my part."

She waved the gun at him. "Oh, now you want to talk to me? That chance has passed. You are finally going to get what's coming to you."

"Don't do this. You're not thinking straight."

"I'm thinking more clearly than I have in a long time. Here's the plan. You're going to sit in the chair behind your desk and then I'm gonna blow your brains all over the back wall of your stupid office that you couldn't even give me a key to." Her hand that was holding the gun began shaking. She steadied it with her other hand and took a deep breath. "Then I'm going to get in my car and go pick up our son at his little girlfriend Claire's house. We are going to get the hell out of this miserable town and never ever have to think about you again!"

Mr. Adams sat down in the chair, his hands stayed raised, the gun still pointed at his head. "Claire isn't his girlfriend, Zellie is, and she's just like Grace."

"What do you mean? She has visions too?" Mrs. Adams narrowed her eyes at her husband. "I don't believe you, Avery wouldn't...he knows that would hurt me."

"It has nothing to do with you. Avery went and fell in love while neither of us was paying attention. We've been awful parents to him. I've neglected him and you've treated him like an adult since he was ten! He needs to get away from Rosedell and I'm going to take him."

He stood up. "Now, you're going to put down that gun and you're going to let me drive you to the hospital. You need some help."

His cell phone began ringing from the front pocket of his jeans. He let it ring.

Mrs. Adams waved the gun toward his pocket. "Take it out and slide it to me across the desk." She pointed the gun back at his head. "Sit down, we're not going anywhere."

He pulled the phone out and slid it to her, she flipped it open, and shut off the phone, tossing it on the floor.

Mr. Adams sat down and put his hands out flat on the desk. He looked his wife in the eye. "Just tell me what I can do."

She backed up, continuing to aim the gun at his head, and slumped down on the couch.

"Grace knew that Erin was going to die, Mike. She knew that Avery wouldn't save her."

He started to get out of the chair, rising slowly. "I know that and I also know she feels just as horrible about it as either of us. There wasn't anything she could do. She--"

"Think about it!" Mrs. Adams got up from the couch and paced back and forth, keeping the gun trained on him. "She knew that my mother was going to have a stroke, that your mother would get breast cancer. Hell, she probably knows how your father, who's all the way in freaking Florida, is going to die and you still love her. You think I'm crazier and more messed up than she is? You're a fool."

"Becky, we never should have gotten married. We had no foundation to build any kind of relationship on, and that's just as much my fault as it is yours. Erin's probably the only thing that could have made us both happy and willing to want to stay together." He had tears in his eyes. "But she's gone. I should have realized that I couldn't be happy without Grace. I don't care what she knows, what she could or couldn't have done. I know that's not fair to you, just like it's not fair to expect Avery to fill the void that Erin left."

Mr. Adams got down on his knees and begged. "Just please let me take our son and give him a clean slate. Let's get you well and I promise I will be in contact with you and you'll see him again." He got up and walked around the desk to his wife. He pushed her hand holding the gun away and embraced her.

She took a deep breath and then put the gun to his chest and pushed him back. "How long have you and the good pastor's wife been sleeping together?"

Mr. Adams closed his eyes and exhaled, defeated.

"You reek of that ridiculous rose perfume that she wears." She shook her head at him. "Didn't think I knew that was going on, did you?"

The saloon doors creaked as they were pulled back and my parents walked in.

Avery snapped his fingers in front of my face.

I came back to reality. "I've got to call my mom right now."

Claire's red glittery cell phone slid across the carpet and hit me in the thigh. I dialed.

"C'mon, c'mon, c'mon," I paced across the room, willing Mom to pick up the phone.

"Hello." Thank God.

"Mom, it's me. Do you know where Dad is?"

"Um...I was sleeping. Hold on, let me see if the minivan is here." I heard her shuffle over to the bedroom window. "Yup. The minivan's parked in the driveway. Do you want me to get him? Are you okay?"

"I have to tell you something. Please don't get mad, okay?"

"I'm listening." I noted that she didn't say she wouldn't get mad.

"I had a vision about Dad, when I hugged him goodbye and then, something else...it was like a vision, but more like I was seeing the immediate future? I don't know, one second I'm talking to Avery about his mom and then--"

"Avery is there?"

"Yes, Mom, Avery is here. Out of all the things I just told you, that's what you're focusing on?"

She took in a deep breath and then let it out. "What did you see, honey? Was it anything like the vision I showed you?"

"In the first one I saw Dad trying to get a gun away from a lady, but she shoots him. In the second whatever, I watched as Avery's mom tried to shoot Avery's dad, but then you and Dad walked into his office."

"Mike Adams office? Oh, God. I didn't have the dream about him last night, Zellie. I can't go near there or he will die for sure." She took another deep breath. "I will keep your dad here and call the police. You have got to have Avery call his father and find out where he is."

"Okay." I paused, and then forced myself to ask, "You're not mad at me?"

Mom started to cry. "We'll talk about this later Zel, go call Mike and find out where he is."

I ended the call with my mom and sat down next to Avery.

"You've got to call your dad and find out where he is." I handed Claire's phone to him. He looked at me, then at the phone and then back to me again like he had forgotten how to use the thing. "Seriously, now. It is very important that we know where your dad is. Something could go down tonight and both of our fathers could end up dead."

Claire finally just came into her bedroom. "Zel, I think he knows he needs to call his father. However, you have just freaked the crap out of me and I'm guessing that he is feeling the same way too. I mean, hello, you have *visions*! How are we supposed to wrap our heads around that and quick like jump on the "Psychic Girl" bandwagon?"

I put one hand on Avery's knee and extended my other to Claire, pulling her down to sit next to us. "Look, I've wanted to tell you both about this, for a while now. It's just that it's weird and confusing and I thought you would think I was crazy." And it would have ruined everything. Crap. It *was* ruining everything. "I thought I had more time."

Claire leaned in and peered into my eyes. "Have you had any visions about me? Do you know when I'm going to die? Am I skinny? Does everyone in the whole town come to my funeral?"

I grinned. Leave it to Claire to bypass the whole weirdness of my abilities and move right on to how it might affect her instead. "No, I haven't seen your death. I haven't had that many visions. Just the ones tonight and the one about..." I turned and looked at Avery, who was staring at me like I was an alien. "...Avery."

He pulled his knees to his chest, letting my hand fall to the floor. I deserved that. "So that's what was happening all those times you were spacing out? You were having visions? Did you have one the first night we got together?"

"Yeah, that was the first one I had." I drew my hands back into my lap. This whole frickin' scene was about to unravel and I didn't have time for it. There was no time to explain myself. "Look, I know you all are freaked out, but this is good. I can stop things before they happen. Avery, I really need you to call your dad and find out where he is. I promise to answer all your questions later, okay?"

He dialed his home phone number and waited for a moment. "The voicemail picked up, my mom's probably still sleeping. I'll try my dad's cell." He punched in the cell number, said hello and then made a weird face. "The phone picked up, but nobody answered it."

I took the phone from him and gave it back to Claire. I could really use a goddamned plan right about now. I chewed my bottom lip furiously. "Do you think he's at his office?"

"I don't know, I mean, he left the house after the fight we had...and if he didn't go back home that's probably where he is."

Standing up, I pulled the other two to their feet. "Okay, here's what we're going to do. Claire, I need to borrow your bike. Avery and I are going to ride over to his dad's office. My mom is calling the police. I'm sure they will be there by the time we get there, but I can't just sit around here and not do anything."

Claire went to her walk-in closet and rummaged around, pulling a teddy bear out from the depths. She unzipped the little satchel on the teddy bear's back and pulled out a key, holding it up to show us. "Zel, you don't have to borrow my bike, we're taking my mom's car. C'mon, I'm driving."

"Have you ever even driven a car before, Claire?" Avery jiggled his leg up and down. Zellie put her hand on his knee to quiet it. He whipped it away from her touch. He just...couldn't, not right now, not with all of the crazy shit she was saying and him not being able to tell if it was true or not. It had to be true, why would she make it all up? But...hell if he could believe anything that came out of her mouth. He had trusted her and she had withheld so much...really important freakin' life altering stuff.

"Uh, yeah, when I was nine my dad let me sit on his lap and steer." Claire looked at him in the rearview mirror. He scowled. "Okay, no jokey time, got it."

He leaned over her shoulder from the back seat. "Could you possibly go any faster than three miles an hour? We could have gotten there quicker if we'd ridden bikes!"

"Sor-ry!" She pushed hard on the brake pedal, jerking the three of them forward. "Oops! Well, let's be thankful it's an automatic or I would have even more pedals to choose from!" She jammed her foot down on the accelerator. "Hey, Zellie, isn't that your dad?"

The Wells' beat up old minivan careened around the corner and sped past them.

"Crap!" Zellie said, looking back as it turned another corner. "Hurry up! We've got to get to Avery's dad before my parents realize that I'm not at your house. If they show up at that office--"

"I know Zellie, people will die." Claire rolled to a near stop at the intersection and jammed on the accelerator again.

She ran three more stop signs, slowing down in front of Adams Insurance, Avery and Zellie were out of the car before she came to a stop. "Hey, wait for me!" she shouted, shoving the car into park and leaving it running in the middle of the street.

Avery had his keys out, fumbling with them to get the door unlocked. He could hear his parents' voices inside the office, but couldn't see anything. All the blinds were drawn. Shit. Zel's effed up vision thing was going to come true and he couldn't make his stupid hands work!

Zellie turned to Claire. "Call the police. They should have been here by now."

Finally steadying his hands enough to unlock the door, Avery stepped inside. His mom turned to face him, her finger on the trigger of a gun. The cow bell on the door clanged as the Wells' minivan tore down the street and rammed into the back of Claire's mother's car.

Chapter Nine

I rushed forward from the sidewalk to the minivan, struggling to open the passenger door, but it wouldn't budge. Mom was slouched against it. Dad's body was hunched over the steering wheel, the air bag smothering him, his chest pressing against the horn. Both of my parents were unconscious, their faces bloody and starting to swell. Smoke billowed from under the hood, a fire had started.

"Mom! Mom! Wake up, can you hear me?" I pulled with all my might against the door. It was no use. I ran around the back of the van to Dad's side. The door opened. Thank you, God. I reached in and pushed him back off of the steering wheel, silencing the horn.

The sound was replaced by screaming. I looked through the smoke to the sidewalk. Claire was lying on the ground passed out. It wasn't her that was screaming. The phone in her slack hand glittered in the bright fluorescent street lights.

Mrs. Adams was the one that was screaming. She stood, static, over Avery with a gun in her hand. He was sprawled out across the threshold of the door, blood erupting from his chest.

I froze, my hand still pressed against Dad's body. My eyes burned like hell, but the tears would not come. I freakin' needed those tears to wash the sight of Avery dying from my eyes. My nostrils stung with pine. Avery. Damn it. Get a hold of yourself, Zellie. Oh, Jesus, Avery! My legs were lead. Where were the police? Someone had to help me!

Staggering into the doorway, Mr. Adams bent down and removed the gun from his wife's hand. Then, absolutely expressionless, he raised it to her head and pulled the trigger.

I wanted to pass out. Wanted to let the pressure of my brain beating against my skull overtake me. I wanted to give up. The pain of losing all of these people at once was too overwhelming.

My body wouldn't give in. I felt my instincts claw their way to the surface, take control. It was like what I felt when I was with Avery, only even more animal, filled with more adrenaline.

I moved forward to the sidewalk. Everything blurred in my periphery, my focus pulled in tight. Hyperaware. Claire's phone lay there glittery, pulsing. I didn't know where Claire had gone. I concentrated on my actions, picked up the phone. Dialed 9-1-1.

"9-1-1, what's your emergency?"

The words were out of my mouth before I thought them. "There's been a really bad car wreck in front of Adams insurance. Cascade Ave. and 2nd St." I hung up. That was all they needed to know. I threw the phone down.

I made eye contact with Mr. Adams. His eyes grew wide as he dropped the gun. I went to him and put my hands on his chest. I could feel his heart surging, overworking itself. I said what I knew was the truth. "It's your day to die."

The gun rose from the sidewalk. It floated in the space between me and Mr. Adams for an instant and then snapped into his hand. The bullet popped out of Mrs. Adams' head and returned to the gun. She sat up, stood and turned towards her husband. He handed her the gun and backed into his office. She followed in the same manner.

I went to Dad in the van, pushed him onto the steering wheel. The horn blaring again. I made my way around to mom, I untried the door. The fire under the hood came to a halt. The pressure in my head was subsiding. I looked around, feeling like I was almost done...

Avery hopped up. The bullet from his chest spun before him and then was whisked into the office. The door closed. He fumbled with his keys.

I ran to him and put my hand on his. It was over now. My mouth was almost too dry to speak, "Stop."

I awoke with a series of sounds ricocheting off the inside of my skull. Cow bell, crash, car horn. Scream, shot, sirens. Over and over again. I opened my eyes, looking to my right and left. There were long white curtains surrounding me. I was in a hospital bed. I had no idea how I had gotten there or what time of day it was.

"Zellie, you awake?"

Melody's face appeared above me, her eyes swollen and red.

"Melody?" I said. My mouth was so dry. "Are Mom and Dad okay?"

"Everyone's...they're all down the hall getting checked out. Mom, Dad, Avery, Claire."

"Avery?" It wasn't a dream. I didn't get knocked on the head or something. He was alive. Oh my God, thank you, thank you. I couldn't catch my breath.

Melody reached down and took my hand. "You saved his life. Don't you remember?"

"What? No, I..." How much did Melody know? I wasn't copping to any memories until I could be sure of what really happened. "Avery's mom accidentally shot him and then his dad shot her, that's the last thing I remember."

"Oh, Zellie," Melody said, tears streaming down her face, pooling at the corners of her upturned mouth. "The visions you have..."

"You know about those?" Claire, damn it, I loved that big-mouthed girl.

She laughed. "Yeah, I do. I always knew you were a freak. But the visions, Zel, they're not the only thing you can do."

I dug my elbows into the hospital bed and pushed myself up to a sitting position. What *had* I done? I tried to summon that feeling again. Raw instinct. It wouldn't come. "Start at the beginning, why were Mom and Dad even there?"

"Well, I was painting my toenails, y'know that one sorta neon green color I got from Britney for my birthday?"

"Melody." I gave her my best exasperated big sister look.

"Jeez. All right! I was painting my toenails in our room and Mom came running down the hall and out the front door screaming after Dad to wait for her. So, I went to the front window to see what the hell was going on and Dad had locked Mom out of the minivan, and she's like, practically ripping the door off and they're yelling at each other, so mad, madder than I've ever seen Dad. He finally lets her in the car and takes off, driving all crazy."

"He must have heard me talking on the phone with Mom and tried to come get me from Claire's."

Melody snorted. "Ya, think?"

"Hey!" I pointed to myself. "Lying in a hospital bed, cut me a break on my slowness."

"Sorry." She shrugged her shoulders. "Everything else I know is all according to Claire, but I have to say that I believe her because a lot of people are alive that shouldn't be. She says that she came to when she heard the gunshot, Mr. Adams shooting Mrs. Adams. She sat up when she realized what had happened and crawled around the corner to take cover."

"Thanks, Melody, I'll take it from here. No need to make me sound like more of a tool than you already were." Claire came to my side, leaned over and kissed me on the forehead. "Welcome back." She had a large white bandage wrapped around her head. She looked like crap.

"Hey. Are you okay?" I asked.

Claire took my hand. "I'm totally fine. You know what they say about short people and their center of gravity being closer to the ground? I'm pretty sure that anyone who breaks their fall with their head gets one of these nifty gauze dealies." She tapped herself on the forehead and then flinched. "I have a wee concussion, some cuts, nothing to worry about. You on the other hand...well, of course you look hot despite your major psychic meltdown, you bitch."

I tested the waters. "You saw everything?"

"If you're referring to how you stopped time and rewound it, then yeah, I saw everything." Claire gave me an exaggerated wink.

Well, forget testing, I guess I was in cannonball territory now. "So what happened after...the rewind? That's the last thing I remember."

"After you passed out?" Claire asked.

I nodded and brought my hand to my head. I was wearing a bandage too. It didn't even hurt. I must be on some serious ibuprofen.

Claire continued. "Your parents got out of the car and ran over to you, and Avery and I, we were all around you. Then Mrs. Adams opened the door of the office and said 'Mike is dead and I didn't kill him.'"

“Avery’s dad is dead?” I sat up. I was going to puke. I remembered the feeling of his heart beating against my palm; I thought it was going to explode out of his chest. “Did I? Oh my God. What did I do to him?”

Claire put a cup of water to my lips and made me take a drink before she answered me. “We don’t know, Zel. Your mom, she ran past Mrs. Adams and checked his pulse and looked him over for signs of injury...but there was nothing. His heart just stopped.

“The ambulance and the police showed up soon after that and tried to revive him, but I guess...your mom’s not handling it too well. Avery either. His mom has totally lost it. The cops took her to the psychiatric hospital over in Bend.”

“What? He’s going to hate me! I ruined his life!” I couldn’t catch my breath. Claire thrust the cup of water into my face again, I pushed her hand away. I threw back the covers on the bed. “I’ve got to see him.”

Claire and Melody both put their hands on my chest and pushed me back down onto the bed. I was too weak to fight them. My breathing started to return to normal.

“You’re not going anywhere. You need to rest.” Claire pulled the curtain shut. She leaned down over me and looked me straight in the eye. “I don’t know how else to put this, but there’s a force inside of you that brought two people back to life and healed your parents to the point that all they have are a couple of scrapes and bruises. That, my friend, can take a lot out of a girl.”

I sunk back into my pillow. “Yes, but I also had to kill someone to make that happen.”

Claire slumped into a chair. The day’s events had taken a lot out of her too. “Zellie, you said it yourself, it was his day to die. I don't think it was you that did anything to him. I think it was meant to be."

Avery was meant to have both of his parents taken away from him in an instant? In what world, to what God was that meant to be? "What does that even mean? How come I didn't heal you, how come you didn't get caught in the rewind? None of this makes sense!"

She grabbed my hand. "I think you knew I wasn't that hurt. I'm glad that I wasn't caught up in it, because I could watch it and tell you what happened. No one else knew what went on until I filled in the details and I'm so glad that I could do that for them and for you." Claire grinned. "I'm like your supernatural sidekick."

Normally, that would have made me smile, but not right now. The weight of the situation suddenly hit me very hard. "Who all knows about this? What did you tell the police?" My actions were going to have consequences. I had possibly killed someone. I could go to jail.

"I told the police that your dad found out that I was driving underage and he'd followed us because he didn't want you in the car with me. Then when he pulled us over, so to speak, I mixed up which was the accelerator and which was the brake. Then I accidentally put the car into reverse instead of drive and I backed up into them pretty hard."

I gave her a "really?" look. She shrugged. "I said I thought that all of us had a nasty case of whiplash, and that I would take full responsibility." Claire sucked in a deep breath. "Then I said that Avery had keys to his dad's office so we all thought that we would go in there and wait for the police.

"But when we went in there, his parents were arguing and his mom had a gun pointed at his dad who proceeded to have a heart attack and that caused extra shock to your system, making you pass out." Claire paused and took another deep breath. "That's my convoluted story and I'm stickin' to it."

"Jesus, Claire. They believed that?" I felt a little more at ease.

"I know!" Melody chimed in. "I could've come up with a more believable cover than that."

Claire shrugged again. "It's a small town. I'm sure our law enforcement is much better equipped to deal with a stupid car accident and a heart attack than the newly revealed powers of Zellie Wells."

"You're probably right." I wasn't even equipped to deal with my...powers. How was any of this real? Visions were one thing, but rewinding time? That was some crazy-ass-super-freakazoid stuff. I looked at Claire; I wasn't the only one who had protected someone's life today. "Thanks for being such a good friend and skilled liar." I reached over to hug her.

As Claire hugged me back she whispered into my ear, "Don't forget, sidekick." She fluffed the pillows around my head. "Now get some sleep and let that IV do its job. Word on the street is you're way dehydrated. I'll see you tomorrow."

She pulled the curtain back from around my bed and left the room. Melody followed her with promises to come back in the morning.

I noticed, for the first time, that there was another patient in the room with me. She was about Mom's age. I don't know how I didn't hear her before. She lay flat on her back snoring with her mouth open. Had she heard what we'd been talking about? She'd have me transferred to the psych ward for sure. I really looked at her and concentrated on her face.

A super bright light shone into her eyes as doctors leaned over her. I could hear metal clinking in the background. One of the doctors adjusted an IV hanging next to her head and then put a mask up to her mouth. "Sarah, I need you to count backwards with me from ten and then we'll get that pesky appendix out and you'll be feeling much better. 10,9,8,7..." She drifted off.

Sarah wasn't waking up for a while and probably didn't hear anything we'd said. Of course, if she had she would most likely chalk it up to a trippy drug induced dream.

I lay back onto my pillows and tried to relax, but my mind was buzzing with questions. What was new about that?

I pictured Avery's face when he'd heard me talking about my visions to Mom and again when I rewound the bullet from his chest. It was the same look, fear and disgust and betrayal.

Now I'd really done it.

And Mom? She probably hated my guts at this moment. Why couldn't I have just listened to her and kept out of the way? I'd only made everything worse by trying to help. Sure, she was alive. Alive to experience the feeling of having her heart and soul ripped from her body.

I didn't want to think about what Dad thought of me. An abomination? A witch? This force inside me went against all of his beliefs.

Which brought me to my other Father. "God," I quietly prayed, "please forgive me. I lost control. I went astray. I know how to do the right thing. I haven't been myself, but I will try. I will try harder than you thought I was capable of."

I wanted to cry. I needed to sob, but I had no tears.

Chapter Ten

I sat in the back pew of the church with Melody and Claire, not even sure I should be at Mr. Adams' funeral, under the circumstances.

It seemed like the whole town was there.

Pastor Morris was leading the service, saying nice things about Mike and Becky Adams both. I knew he was trying to help Avery deal with the tremendous loss he had suffered at my hand.

Jason's dad, Ray Erickson, gave the eulogy. He placed one hand on Mr. Adams' casket and rubbed the tears from his eyes with the other. "Mike and I have been buddies since kindergarten. A long time." He knocked twice on the casket. "But not long enough, man." His voice cracked. He wiped his eyes again. "But our boys Mikey, they'll carry it on." He looked at Jason, "I love you, Son."

Avery sat in the front row staring straight ahead. I watched the light shining through the stained glass windows play upon the silvery hairs that had sprouted all over his head. No one would ever see him look like a teenager again. In the three days that had passed since his dad's death and his mom being committed, Avery looked like he had aged years. To me, he was more beautiful than ever. I was sure it was Nature's way of punishing me.

My parents sat next to him in the front pew. Mom had her arm around his shoulders and Dad's arm was around hers.

Ray pulled himself together. "Gracie," he looked to Mom. She sobbed in acknowledgement. Dad removed his arm from around her shoulders. "Gracie, we've lost our friend, but for the kid's sake we gotta keep his memory alive."

She nodded, squeezed Avery's arm. "I hear ya Ray. He'll always be with me. He's not easy to forget."

Ray chuckled, wiped his nose. "Mike, Becky, Gracie and I, we used to tear it up, y'know? I'm sure some of you older folks remember?"

"Tell the story about the rodeo!" a man my parents age yelled from the middle of the church.

Ray nodded his head, obliging. "This one time, we crashed the Labor Day rodeo. Drunker than skunks, and Mike, that son of a gun..." He gestured putting on a cowboy hat. "He stole a clown costume, this huge cowboy hat and pants. He and Gracie both got in the pants, Mike put on the hat and Gracie had a handkerchief around her neck...each with a suspender on their shoulder...they just ran right out into the middle of the Little Miss Rosedell competition." He broke out into a hearty laugh.

"All these cute little made up girls, twirling their batons, doin' their line dance routines. Aw, man, it was hilarious." He sighed and knocked on the casket again. "I'm going to miss you brother." He pointed up in the air and then brought his hand into a fist and kissed it.

He walked down the three steps from the altar to the pews and then back up again. "I almost forgot." Ray pulled a gold pin from the inside pocket of his suit jacket and held it up for everyone to see. "This is a pin with the 519 insignia on it. My guys over at the firehouse thought Mike should be buried with it. It's in recognition of his twenty-four years as a volunteer firefighter." He placed the pin on top of the casket and walked back down the stairs towards Mom.

She stood up and leaned over the pew, grabbing Ray in sturdy hug, kissing him on the cheek and then rubbing her lipstick from his face with her thumb. Ray shook Dad's hand and then took Avery's hand and pulled him up into big, back slapping embrace.

It was like Avery was everyone's kid now and Mom was Mr. Adams' widow. I had no idea where that left me or Dad in the equation. My parents hadn't really spoken to me since I'd been released from the hospital.

The morning after the accident, when the doctors deemed me healthy and hydrated, I'd walked with my parents in silence from the hospital to the maroon car they'd rented. Melody and Claire were doing the welcome home dance when we pulled into the driveway, but stopped abruptly when Mom burst into tears and Dad stormed into the house.

If it weren't for Claire and Melody, I would be all alone. At least I knew why Mom was mad at me. She'd thrown the green letter in my face, saying, "You might want to try and follow the rules."

This had made me furious because, after really thinking the situation through, I mean, under the circumstances could it have gone any other way? Should I have left everyone dead and injured? And for that matter, I didn't even know what I was doing when I saved everyone else's life by taking Mr. Adams'.

Dad was a different story. He acted like he was afraid of me, like he didn't know who I was. I guess I should be lucky he still let me live under his roof.

The worst part was that I expected things to be like this, but was hopeful that I was overreacting. Losing that hope, it made me mad as hell. And that made me feel guilty and contrite and confused all over again.

Pastor Morris spoke. “Can the pallbearers please come forward?”

Dad, Jason and Ray Erickson, a few other men, walked somberly to the front of the church, stationed themselves around Mr. Adams' casket and hoisted it up onto their shoulders. Avery and Mom followed behind them.

As the men carried the casket down the aisle, Pastor Morris instructed everyone to follow the hearse out to Rosedell cemetery for the interment and to please remember to turn their headlights on.

We all stood as the pallbearers passed. I forced myself to make eye contact with Avery. It was not returned.

After the funeral, as if the situation wasn't awkward enough, my parents invited everyone to come back to our house for a bite to eat and to pay their condolences to Avery.

I tried to help Mom in the kitchen, setting out cold cuts on a platter, but I seemed to be in her way no matter where I stood or what I did. “I think you've done enough already,” she hissed at me under her breath.

Exiled from the kitchen, I went into the living room. Avery was in there sitting on the couch, looking uncomfortable. People kept hugging him.

Now was my chance. With all of these people here, maybe he would listen to me. I sat down next to him. “Avery. I'm so sorry.” I reached out for his hand.

He leaned away from me and then stood up. “Don't Zel. Not now.”

My eyes went blank, the Avery vision overtaking me.

I came to; he was snapping his fingers in my face. "Nice. You can't cut that shit out for one day?" He took off out the front door.

Everyone was staring at us. Ugh! My house was too crowded, I felt like I couldn't breathe. Every time I brushed shoulders with an elderly person, and there were plenty of them there, I got a quick flash of them dying or dead. Mostly of natural causes, thank God. I hoped that this particular new development went away, no wonder my grandma killed herself.

I went into my bedroom. Mel and Claire were already hiding in there, sitting on Melody's bed.

"Hey." I flopped down on my bed, flinging my arm across my face. "Is this day ever going to end?"

Claire switched beds and plunked down next to me, cuddling up. "It's got to." She played with my hair, letting it run through her fingers. "Listen, we've been talking. How about the three of us go stay with your Aunt Hazel for the summer? Just the summer. Give people some time to get their heads out of their asses and love you again."

I sat up and looked across the room at my sister. "What exactly did you tell Claire about Aunt Hazel that would make her think that would be a good idea?"

Melody looked down at her hands, picking some nail polish from her thumb. "She lives in Portland, that's what I told her. Zellie, every year in her Christmas cards she always tells us that we're welcome to stay with her. I can't think of a better time."

"Isn't Aunt Hazel like, sixty years old though? I mean, three teenage girls in her one bedroom apartment for a whole summer? I don't think that's the kind of visit she was envisioning."

Melody got up and walked to the edge of my bed. I had never seen her so serious. Ever.

"I read the letter that Mom gave you and I called Aunt Hazel already. I told her everything." She teared up. "She said it was my responsibility to take care of you right now, she said that we younger sisters may not have the powers that you and Grandma did, but that we were meant to be your protectors. And that's what I'm going to do Zellie, so, no more talking about this. Mom and Dad think it's a good idea too. We leave the day after tomorrow. Claire's dad is going to drive us."

"Okay," I said simply, realizing I had nothing keeping me here.

I stood outside in the driveway waiting for Mr. Vargas to come pick us up. Melody was still packing.

It was a perfect summer day. The sky was a crisp cloudless blue and the heat had let up a little for once. I closed my eyes and turned my face upward, soaking in the sun. Hearing a car pull into the gravel driveway, I opened my eyes, expecting to see Mr. Vargas' immense green Suburban.

Instead, it was Mr. Adams' red truck with Avery behind the wheel.

He turned off the ignition and jumped down from the truck, pointing his key chain and pressing a button to lock the doors.

I fought the urge to run back into the house and hide in my room as he walked toward me. I scrambled for something insignificant to say. "Hey, you're not supposed to be driving yet!" I turned the corners of my mouth up, attempting to be cheerful.

He stuffed the keys into his jeans pockets. "Yeah, well there isn't anybody to tell me not to so..."

I dropped the corners of my mouth. "Right, sorry. I wasn't thinking."

He stood stock still in front of me, as beautiful as ever. His hair was pretty long now, curling way over his ears. He never did get that haircut from his mom. I ached in every part of my body.

"I have some things I need to say to you before I lose my nerve," he said.

"Okay." I could barely get the word out of my throat.

Avery steeled himself and looked me straight in the eye. "I know you didn't kill my dad on purpose. I know that you were trying to save him. That you thought my mom was going to kill him because of the vision you had or whatever...but then you're saying you had a vision of your dad dying too."

"Avery. I'm so sorry. You have to know that--" I felt like I was going to collapse.

He held his hand up to stop me talking and took a deep breath in. "What I wanna know is, what made it more my dad's day to die than yours?"

I couldn't get the words out fast enough now. "I don't know. Don't you think I've thought about that too? Believe me when I say that I don't know what came over me. I don't even have theories. All of this? This vision stuff? It's only been happening to me for a couple of months."

Avery looked away, blinking back tears. "So that's all you have to say? You don't know?"

That got me crying too. He wasn't going to hear me out. "Yes, for now that's all I can say. I'm hoping my aunt

Hazel can help me fill in the blanks. Especially since my own mom isn't speaking to me."

He glared at me. "Can you really blame her? My dad was the love of her life." Avery wiped his forearm across his eyes. "You know, I thought you were going to be that for me? That's all screwed up now isn't it?"

"Yeah, I guess it is." My blood began to boil. This boy had no forgiveness inside him and it was pissing me off.

"Avery, I have a question for you. Why can't we blame her? Why can't we blame them? If your dad had never talked my mom into moving back here, none of this would have happened." I reached out to touch his arm; I needed him to remember our bond.

He flinched, stepping back from me. "Don't touch me, please."

Oh, I'd had enough of this. If he wanted to throw what was between us away, well then I was gonna help him do it. I pushed him as hard as I could. I wanted him with me or gone! He stumbled backwards and fell.

"Come off it, Avery!" I yelled. "God! You know what? You, my parents, you can all just go to hell."

He stayed on the ground, looking like he was terrified of what I might do next.

Now I was hollering. "I saved your lives. When is that going to register with any of you? You would be *dead* now if it weren't for me. This whole stupid vision thing? It's trial and error, but I have had nothing but good intentions. I lied a minute ago. It was your dad's day to die, regardless of whether I intervened or not. Regardless of what I did or did not do. It was either going to be me that killed him or your mom that did."

I balled my fists up, feeling like I was going to bust wide open. "I mean, if your mom had killed your dad, no one would be mad at me right?" I leaned down and got in his face. "No. Wrong. Because if you'd found out after the fact that I could have done something and didn't, you would have hated me more than you do now. My dad was not supposed to be there Avery, and yours was."

Kneeling down, I made a last ditch effort and reached for him. Why wouldn't he understand? Why wouldn't he love me in spite of everything?

Avery dodged my grasp and got to his feet, pulling his keys from his jeans pocket. "Wow. I didn't know you could be such a bitch, Zellie. I can't believe that I was ever in love with you."

He turned away from me and walked back to his truck. Over his shoulder he said, "I hope you get some answers, I really do. But don't bother telling me. We're done. I'm never going to forgive you, you stupid freak."

I picked up a handful of gravel and flung it at him, hitting the open driver's side door. "Yeah, we'll see about that!" I screamed, "Don't forget I still have to save your dumb ass sometime in the future!" I crumpled and fell forward onto the palms of my hands, sobbing.

Avery started up the truck, flipped me off, and drove away.

Melody rolled one of her three suitcases down the steps. "Is everything okay out here? I saw you push him down. That was awesome."

"No." I got up, brushing the rock dust from my knees.

Melody stood beside me. "Everything gonna be okay?"

I turned to her, a weak smile on my face. "Honestly, Mel, I don't know. That's not the kind of future I can see."

Chapter Eleven

Aunt Hazel was nice enough to us, but made it clear early on that she did and had everything the way she liked it. Also, there was a time and a place to discuss my visions, which was over dinner at exactly six every night. Other than that, she wanted us girls out of the apartment taking advantage of all that Portland had to offer.

Three weeks into our stay, we'd developed a sort of routine. We woke every morning at eight, showered, dressed, ate a piece of toast and walked from Aunt Hazel's apartment to the MAX train. So far we'd been to the zoo, downtown, and out to the airport for some people watching. But mostly we just went to Lloyd Center.

I welcomed the routine. The normality of being a sixteen-year-old girl who hangs out at the mall buying bulk candy and riding escalators all day long felt good.

I wasn't getting a ton of answers from my great-aunt about the visions, but I was starting to welcome that too. Our dinner conversations were more about Aunt Hazel regaling us with stories of all the people Grandma had saved with her abilities, than answers.

Melody crammed her fiftieth sour gummy worm of the day into her mouth as we boarded the MAX. She had changed a lot for the better. For one, she was moderately nice to me. For another, it seemed like being popular was the furthest thing from her mind anymore.

"You know we're having dinner in half an hour, Mel," I said, "Aunt Hazel's going to be pissed if you don't eat any of her fabulous cuisine." I giggled, reaching into Melody's bag of candy.

Claire took a chocolate bar from her slouchy green handbag. "Yeah, it's Tuna Tuesday, what are you thinking?"

Melody snagged the only open seat in the compartment, holding her stomach. "I'm thinking I can either barf from all of the candy or barf from the tuna casserole and I'm going with the candy."

The business man seated next to her got up from his seat and went to stand by the door.

"Good call," Claire said, taking the man's seat.

We got off the MAX two stops later and climbed the hill to Aunt Hazel's. She lived on Burnside in the top floor apartment of a yellow house. There were two apartments downstairs occupied by ladies even older than her. Claire had taken to calling it the "Happy Haven Retirement Home."

"Hey, whose Beemer is that parked in front of the Haven?" Claire said as we came to the top of the hill.

"Hmm, I don't know. Maybe one of the other residents has a rich son visiting," I said.

We rounded the corner and faced the house.

Melody pointed to Aunt Hazel's apartment. "No, I don't think so. Look, there's a lady standing at the window staring at us."

We all looked up at her. Claire waved and the lady waved back. "Cool, a dinner guest."

Aunt Hazel met us at the top of the stairs. She nervously tucked a lock of her bobbed grey hair behind her ear. "Hi, girls, I hope you had a good day. I've...we've got a guest for dinner tonight. Actually, she's going to be staying with us for a while." She ushered us through the door into the apartment.

A tall red headed woman turned from the kitchen window and smiled.

Claire gasped. "Hey, I...you're the lady from the dressing room in Bend when we went to get dresses for Zellie's party!"

"Yes, Claire, that was me." She stepped toward us, her hand extended. "Hello, Zellie. Hello, Melody. It's nice to meet you." She took my hand and a thousand images from my family's life flashed in my mind. "I'm Rachel Loughlin, your dead grandmother."

Melody turned to me and slugged me on the arm. "You really can't see stuff like this coming? Your powers suck."

Tears welled in my eyes. "Melody, how many times do I have to tell you? This isn't the kind of future I can see!"

Grandma put her hand on my shoulder, her eyes bright, "Let's see if we can't do something about that."

The three of us girls sat huddled on Aunt Hazel's orange floral couch while the two older women sat opposite us on vinyl kitchen chairs.

"You're definitely our grandma?" Melody asked.

"Yes." Grandma thought for a moment. "If you need proof, I believe you have a letter on green paper that I wrote to your mother? Explaining why I killed myself?"

"Uh huh, and what exactly happened there?" Mel was not going to let Grandma off easy. I was grateful that she could pull herself together enough to get some answers, I sure as hell couldn't.

"Hazel and I faked my death," she said matter-of-factly. "Your great-aunt was the one who gave your mom the letter." Grandma sighed. "I thought that your mother would have a better chance at a normal life if I wasn't around. People in Rosedell were starting to become very suspicious of me and your mother bore the brunt of that."

I was so familiar with the look Grandma had on her face. It said, "Please just believe me, I'm not sure of anything and I pretty much end up ruining everyone's life."

She continued trying to explain herself. "People said I was a witch, that I was possessed, nonsense like that. I knew that I wouldn't and didn't want to stop acting on my visions. Around that time I was contacted by the head of the West Coast branch of The Society. They had seen what I was doing in Rosedell and recruited me to work for them. So, I moved to Los Angeles. There, I am more anonymous, and therefore able to help a greater number of people."

"What's The Society?" Claire asked.

"It's an organization of women like me, like Zellie and Grace, that has been around for hundreds of years."

"Why are we only meeting you now?" Melody was full of questions. I couldn't seem to make my mouth work.

"I check up on you periodically. Hazel keeps up with you in the normal fashion. I concentrate on your mother when she dreams at night. Then I can see what she sees."

After all that she had heard, Melody still seemed skeptical. I didn't blame her; she hadn't been caught up in my scary-ass rewind like everyone else. The reality of my powers hadn't slammed into her full force.

Grandma tried speaking to me now. "For instance, the night of your birthday," she smiled, "I assume that was the first time you had the Avery vision?"

"Uh, yeah," I said, my stomach flip-flopping at the mention of his name.

"That night I concentrated on what your mother was dreaming and she'd seen the vision and so I, in turn, saw it too."

"That doesn't really explain why we're meeting you now." Melody eyed her, suspicious.

Grandma grinned, turning to Aunt Hazel. "She is such a Lookout!"

"I know." Aunt Hazel actually started clapping with excitement. "I think she's going to be great!"

"I'm a what?" Melody leaned forward.

"A Lookout," Aunt Hazel explained. "The older sister is almost always the seer, while the younger sister, like you and me Melody, we're what's known as the Lookout. We aid and to a certain extent, protect the seer."

"What about me?" Claire asked, "Do I get a cool name too?"

Grandma grinned again. "I believe your title would be BFF."

"Of course I don't get a cool name," Claire muttered.

I finally got my words to catch up with my thoughts. "I'm a seer? There's a name for it? I have visions about when people are going to die."

"Among other things," Grandma interjected.

"Among other things...that I haven't learned how to do yet?" I asked. There was more to this? I wasn't even sure that I wanted the abilities I knew about, let alone new ones.

"Precisely," Grandma said.

"But you're going to teach me how to use them, uh, do them? Whatever them?"

"Yes. That's what I'm here for. Actually, Zellie, you're more appropriately called a Retroact. I'm one also. That's what we call someone who can stop and reverse time."

I might as well come clean with her now, she probably knew about Avery's dad anyway. "I still ended up killing Mr. Adams," I confessed.

"No, you didn't." She shook her head. "That's a misconception. Mike died of a heart attack. We can't use our abilities to harm."

"So...I didn't do anything to him? But I touched his chest, I felt his heart surge. I plain as day told him it was his day to die!"

Grandma shook her head "no."

I felt a wave of relief wash over me. "I've got to call Mom right now. She has to know." I got up, totally flustered and downright ecstatic. "Avery. He'll forgive me now."

Grandma stood, putting her hand up to stop me from going to the phone. "I don't think that's a good idea yet. They both need more time to grieve. When they're ready,

I hope to clear up that problem for you." We both sat back down, only now I was all hyper and on the edge of my seat.

Melody was skeptical. "And how are you gonna do that?"

"Your mother doesn't have the exact abilities as your sister and I." Grandma turned to me. "That's why her visions started later, because she's not a Retroact. There are several different types of seers and I'm willing to bet, although her powers are fairly latent, that she is capable of communicating with spirits."

"And what's the cool name for that?" Claire retorted.

"There isn't one." Grandma shrugged.

"You're going to somehow help Mom talk to Mr. Adams and he's going to, what, explain everything?" I asked. I did not think that was going to work worth a damn.

"Essentially." Her gaze softened. "One of the things I'm going to teach you to do is to control your visions so that you can get a glimpse of the future. It's not one hundred percent accurate, especially when you're new. However, I've been doing this awhile and I have a pretty good track record. I've seen your mother talking to Mike. I think she just needs to know that the possibility exists and then she'll be a quick study."

"But it's not one hundred percent?" I said.

"The future is always changing, Zellie, in the smallest ways. The visions are accurate enough to, at the very least, get a broad picture of events and outcomes. Don't be so distressed. You'll learn to trust the visions, I promise."

"Wait. I think I've done this glimpse thing already. You're saying I can do it on purpose?"

She smiled. "You'll be able to use all of your abilities on purpose when I'm done teaching you."

"So, everything is going to end up okay? What about Dad?" I asked. When we left Rosedell, Dad had been crying like I'd never seen him cry before. He'd given me a hug and told me that he loved me, but probably because he had to, not because he wanted to.

"You're father's going to be a bit of a holdout, which, frankly, amuses me to no end." Grandma smirked. "If a man can believe in a God he doesn't see, then how hard is it to accept that he has magically gifted female relatives?"

Melody lashed out. "If you're so great and know how everything's going to turn out, then why didn't you come sooner? We could've avoided this whole horrible mess."

The smirk dropped from Grandma's face. "I got too wrapped up in the last case I was on. I just didn't think to see if you needed my help as often as I should have."

Now I was starting to get pissed off. She could be kind of a selfish old lady. “Grandma, I think I can safely say that Mom could have used your help. We all could have used your help.”

She cringed. “I know that now. I was naïve in thinking that my leaving your mom was for the best. But I left her in good hands. There has been little to worry about all these years. Even after I met others of our kind in The Society, and learned the rules and guidelines, I still really believed that your mother had done enough to prevent Mike’s death.”

She folded her hands in her lap and lowered her voice. “I became a little unsure that all was well after I saw your vision through Grace’s eyes. But when I eavesdropped on your conversation in Bend--”

“Yeah, what was up with that?” Claire asked. “If you can see the future and watch people’s dreams, then why go old school and eavesdrop?”

Grandma stood and began pacing around the room. “The closer I am the easier it is for me to get an accurate reading.” She smiled at Claire. “You girls were so funny. I enjoyed listening to you and didn’t get a bad feeling about Zellie’s future with Avery at all.” She shrugged her shoulders. “After she started having visions I knew that I needed to be here to guide her because Grace wasn’t capable.” She ran her fingers through her hair. “I thought I was going to have more time to plot my return and ease you all into this.”

Well, okay, I could understand thinking you had more time to deal than you actually did.

Melody’s stomach growled.

“Perhaps we should eat dinner? It’s Tuna Tuesday!” Aunt Hazel said.

"Wait. One more question." For some reason I raised my hand like I was in school. "Why did the visions start with Avery?" If Grandma hadn't had a bad feeling...maybe there was a chance to salvage my relationship with him after all.

Grandma stopped and looked at Aunt Hazel, a strange expression on her face. "Hmm, that's a bit of a delicate subject and another reason I thought I had more time."

Oh God. It was something awful. "Just tell me," I said, bracing myself for the Apocalypse.

Grandma started pacing again. "I used to believe that the visions were triggered by the first person you fell in love with. That would be true for me and while your mother loves your father now, Mike was the first man she loved."

She avoided making eye contact with me. "However, on speaking with other seers in The Society, the consensus is that the trigger person is actually...the individual you have a strong physical connection to, not necessarily the first person you love."

Claire and Melody turned to look at me so fast I could hear their necks crack.

I was beyond mortified. "What?"

"Dude, did you and Avery...?" Claire said.

"No!" I turned seven different shades of red.

Claire's eyes got wide. "But it was only a matter of time?"

I didn't answer. I was not going there with my mind-reading grandma and super nosy aunt in the room.

Melody intervened. "Well, there's no way that anything is going to happen now, not after he called her a stupid freak." She snorted. "He's such a buttwipe."

Grandma went into the kitchen. She started spooning casserole into bowls.

Mel put her arm around my shoulders. "So, let's hear some more about this Lookout thing."

Aunt Hazel also seemed eager to move away from the discussion of my chastity. "The Lookout creates cover stories, asks questions, and brings attention to herself. For example, in January, we had a case in San Francisco--"

"San Francisco? You work in California too, Aunt Hazel?" Melody was impressed.

"Yes, we have several residences up and down the West Coast that we all share, depending on who is working on what case. We spend a good amount of time in Los Angeles. It's what you might call home base."

Grandma came back into the room and handed out bowls of food with forks sticking up out of them. She sat back down in her kitchen chair.

Aunt Hazel took a hearty bite. "So, as I was saying, there was a woman in San Francisco that Rachel had seen being carjacked in a parking garage. Then she was forced to drive out to the country by this man, where he raped her."

She leaned forward, getting into it. "Now, sometimes we can get to the scene before anything has happened. With this case, the carjacking was already in progress. So, while I made sure that no one was watching Rachel, she rewound the scene back to before the woman entered the parking garage. I called 9-1-1 and reported a car theft. When we heard the authorities coming, your grandma made a quick getaway as I watched the police catch the man breaking into the woman's car."

She took another bite. "After his apprehension, it was discovered that he was a serial rapist who had been terrorizing women in the area for several months."

"What happened to the woman? Did she remember being rewound?" I asked. I'd never had the chance to discover if the people I'd rewound knew what happened to them or how it felt.

"Usually, people are aware that something has happened to them. For instance, this woman came out to the parking garage and there's a scary man with a gun being arrested for breaking into her car. But, people don't trust their own minds a lot of the time. They're quick to forget the specifics of being rewound."

Melody was following the story intently. "What about video surveillance in the parking garage? How do you get around stuff like that?"

"Good question, Melody. That can be a tricky situation. Most of the time--"

"Interesting," Claire interrupted, "Now, can we get back to this Avery and Zellie doing it thing?"

"Ugh! Leave it alone!" I reached around Melody and slugged Claire on the shoulder.

"What! You don't wanna know if psychic granny here has seen what's going to happen with you guys?"

All three of us girls looked to Grandma. She held her fork to her mouth, about to take a bite. "I haven't tried to see and I won't unless you want me to, dear."

I glared at Claire. "I'm not ready to go there yet."

Claire pouted. "How could you possibly not want to know? I just don't get it."

Fine, I'll tell her the truth. Maybe then she'll shut up about it. "He triggered the visions, but that doesn't mean that it was love, okay? Get it?" I leaned my head back and forced the tears I could feel coming back in. "Avery doesn't love me anymore and he doesn't have to for this stuff to work." I looked at Grandma. "So, if that's what the future holds, I don't really want to know."

Grandma nodded her head. "Fair enough." She set her bowl down on the floor. "That's plenty of questions for tonight. What do you say we do something normal? *Big Brother's* going to be on soon."

At six the next morning Grandma shook me awake. "Come on, we've got a lot of work to do. Get dressed. I've put the kettle on for tea."

I scooted to the edge of the pull-out couch I shared with Melody. I tried not to step on Claire, who slept on an air mattress positioned between the couch and a closet door. Our sleeping arrangements took up almost the entire floor of the family room. I made my way into the bathroom, brushed my teeth, washed my face and threw on the only clean outfit left in my suitcase.

Grandma was waiting for me when I opened the bathroom door. She had two insulated mugs in the crook of one arm and her large brown purse in the opposite hand. "Ready?" she whispered. "Let's walk over to the MAX station. I try to take the light rail when I'm in Portland. Parking downtown," she rolled her eyes, "there's always construction."

We stepped outside. It was already muggy. July was the worst. It never cooled down past seventy at night and with our close proximity to the Willamette River, moisture clung to the air. I pushed the sleeves of my pullover up to my elbows. "What are we doing today, Grandma?"

She handed me a mug. "I thought we'd go downtown. Try and find you someone to rewind."

"I don't know." I took a drink of tea. "The last time I did a rewind I ended up in the hospital."

"That's because your ability had to work without your consent. When your intention is to rewind, the process doesn't take so much out of you." She nodded toward my tea. "Still, you'd better drink up."

We descended the stairs to the MAX platform and sat on a metal bench under an overhang. While we waited for the next westbound train, Grandma dug in her bag. She tore a prepaid ticket from a book and gave one to me.

"Here we go." She stood up and walked to the edge of the platform. I followed. We boarded a car with two seating areas, one on the level we were standing on, and another up three steps. Grandma chose to sit on the lower level facing towards the upper level.

When the MAX started moving, she leaned in to me and spoke in a hushed tone. "Okay. What do you feel about the blonde woman sitting on the upper level there, with the red shirt?"

I was confused. "What do I feel about her?" I studied her for a moment, nothing popped into my head. "I don't get a reading on her, if that's what you mean. I think I'm better at guessing after they've already gotten sick or hurt themselves."

"Focus, really try to see it happening."

The MAX slowed down and the woman got up, walking toward us to the steps. The vision clicked in my head. I leapt forward from my seat and caught her by the arm just as she slipped down the steps. "Watch it now!" I said, helping her to her feet.

"Thank you. I just about bit it big time, didn't I?" She giggled.

"Yeah, you might wanna rethink those high heels. You're liable to break an ankle."

The MAX came to a stop and the doors opened. The woman got off the car, giving me a little wave. "Thanks again."

I sat back down next to Grandma. "How was that? I thought just plain helping her was easier than trying to rewind her fall."

She put a finger to her lips and patted my knee. "That was great. You're right about not rewinding, far too many people and neither one of us has our Lookouts."

"So, is Aunt Hazel going to be giving Melody lessons too?" I whispered.

She nodded. "Just as soon as one of us has a vision that deserves the full treatment."

We crossed Steel Bridge. I looked down at the water. I'd liked helping that lady, keeping her from breaking her ankle. I concentrated on the boats below. Everything seemed to be going well, which was good I supposed. That thought made me get the giggles.

Grandma patted my knee again. "I know you're anxious to get started Zellie, but let's try and not wish someone were drowning."

The MAX made a stop in Old Town. Grandma nudged me with her purse. "This is where we get off."

I followed her from the MAX down an alley between a strip club and a Chinese restaurant. What? Your grandma doesn't hang out in places like that too? It was kind of gross.

"This is usually a reliable place to find a few drunks napping. You can practice your rewinds here." Grandma stood and pointed to the end of the alley where three dumpsters sat all askew.

I didn't walk any further. "You want me to practice on drunks?" That was way icky, morally speaking.

Grandma threw her hands up. "It's either that or coma patients, and half the time they wake up after being rewound. Drunks ask fewer questions."

I sighed. "All right, how do I start?"

She walked toward one of the dumpsters and peered inside. "I'm going to lift this gentleman out and then you can put him back in." She held her arm out. "It helps if you channel the energy through your fingers. Try it, you'll feel what I mean. Concentrate. Focus on your intention. See the rewind happening." She spread her fingers apart, lifted her arm up, summoning.

Two dirty bare feet rose into the air and out over the dumpster, bending the man they were attached to over the edge. Grandma flicked her wrist back. The man's toes found their way to the ground. He stood up. She held him there. "Okay. I've got him. Now, you help him back in." She nodded at the dumpster.

"This has totally got to be illegal," I muttered. I put my hand out in front of me and focused. I pictured the man floating, moving upward. He lifted a foot.

Grandma stepped away, her arm down at her side. "That's it, easy now."

The man didn't move. I tightened my focus. Uh-oh. Pine. I struggled to hold onto him. "Grandma, I'm about to..."

He was sitting at a long cafeteria table in a gymnasium eating chicken and noodles off of a paper plate, looking a little cleaner than he did now. His chin-length gray hair was combed back out of his face and he had different clothes on, jeans and a white Blazers t-shirt. Another man came up behind him, staggering and dragging his left foot.

"Hey. David. You gonna pretend you don't know me?" the man said.

David turned away from his food, terror in his eyes, and looked back. The other man jammed a pocket knife into his neck. Blood poured down David's chest, soaking his shirt.

I snapped back. David lay on the ground against the wall, his knees tucked up to his chest. Grandma took her cell phone out and held it up. "Do I need to call Hazel and Melody?"

Why does everyone have a cell phone but me? "Yeah," I said. "Do you have a camera on that thing? You might want to get a picture of him."

Grandma aimed her phone at David. He stretched his legs out straight and rolled over, facing the wall. She tiptoed past him and hooked her arm with mine, pulling me out to the street.

I looked back. "Shouldn't we warn him or something?"

She shook her head. "It's against The Society's rules I'm afraid. We can prevent, but not warn. It helps us keep a low profile." She took my hand, closed her eyes and saw the David vision. "Stabbing. Those are always so bloody. Let's get back to the apartment." She led me back to the MAX.

Waiting, Grandma called Aunt Hazel.

"Zellie's had a vision," she said, muted. "We're getting on the MAX now. We'll be home in twenty minutes. Wake the other girls up if you haven't already."

When we arrived at the apartment, there was a dry erase board set up in the family room. Melody jumped up from the couch, taking the cap off of the blue marker in her hand. "Tell me every detail. I've totally got this."

I walked past her to the bathroom. "Hold on, I'm sweating to death." I dug around in one of Melody's suitcases. "Can I wear your green tank top?" I called to her, ripping the pullover off and putting the tank top on before she could answer.

"I guess. Hurry up!"

I came back into the room. "Okay. Details..." I paced, while Melody wrote. Aunt Hazel, Grandma, and Claire all sat on the couch, observing. I felt like Mel and I were teaching a seminar in freakanomics. "His name is David. He's homeless. He's got gray hair. Skinny. In the vision he was wearing light blue jeans and a white Blazers t-shirt. Grandma's got a picture on her cell."

Melody looked at me. "Grandma's got a cell phone? Seriously?" She glanced at the phone Grandma held up. "What else, Zellie?"

I ran my fingers through my hair. "Let's see. He was in a gymnasium, but it was set up like a soup line or a shelter. Eating chicken and noodles I think? I didn't focus on getting a good look at the other guy, the one who stabbed him. Did you, Grandma?"

She closed her eyes. "Short. Wearing a baseball cap, pulled down. Mariners colors. Black polo shirt. He's white. That's all I can see."

"What else do we need to know, Aunt Hazel?" Melody asked.

"Those are some really good details. What do you think should be our next step, Melody?"

She scanned the dry erase board. "The next thing I would do is call local aid organizations and find out if they serve their meals in a gym. That right there makes me think it's a church school thing, like St. Mary's in Rosedell.

"Then I need to narrow the list down further to places with a preplanned menu and find out what day they're serving what David was eating." She chewed her bottom lip, contemplating the board again. "I'm assuming it's local because they're probably both homeless and...I'm thinking it's all going to go down soon because they're dressed for warm weather."

"Crackerjack!" Aunt Hazel said, "Let's you and I get started calling places." She took the phone book from the drawer in the telephone table and handed Melody the cordless phone.

Claire got up from the couch, mouthing "crackerjack?" to me. What can I say; Aunt Hazel was a little weird.

"I'm going to step outside and call my parents," Claire said, "I'll be right back."

I turned to Grandma. "What do we do now?" I rocked back and forth on the balls of my feet, hyperactive as all get out.

"We let our Lookouts do their job." She got up and came to me, putting her arm around my shoulders. "You're doing great. I wish we would've been able to practice rewinding, but this is where we're needed, I guess. Are you up for trying to get a glimpse of the future?"

My stomach spoke up.

Grandma smiled, "After breakfast then? We never did eat those bagels I brought with me this morning." She picked her purse up from the couch and extracted a brown paper sack.

"Mm, purse bagels," I said, holding out my hands.

Avery stared at his bedroom ceiling listening to the phone ring, hoping Mrs. Wells would answer it. When she hadn't picked up after the sixth ring, he grabbed the phone and hit TALK. "Hello?"

"Hey Avery, its Claire, how's it goin'?"

He looked at the clock on his bedside table. 8:30. She was awfully damn chipper for this early in the morning on summer vacation. "Fine, what's up?"

"Well, I know that you didn't want Zellie to tell you what she found out, but...there are a lot of things you need to know, man."

"Like what?" He snorted, trying to sound like his stomach hadn't dropped at the mention of Zellie's name. "Are any of these things going to bring my dad back or make my mom less crazy?"

"Maybe," she said quickly. "I mean...Mrs. Wells? Okay, don't spaz, but she can communicate with your dad's spirit."

Sure she could. The only thing Mrs. Wells was capable of communicating with at this juncture was a box of Kleenex. "What the hell are you talking about, Claire?"

"She doesn't know that she can do it, but she can. You need to tell her to focus, to concentrate. That seems to be the key with all of the abilities."

"Yeah, I'm going back to bed now." He should've known better than to answer the phone in the first place, she was dredging up feelings he wasn't ready to deal with.

"No! Avery, wait!" she yelled.

"What? Get to the point or I'm hanging up."

"All right, all right!" She paused as if trying to decide what to tell him. "The most important thing I've learned is that Zellie didn't do anything to your dad."

"Really?"

"Really. There is absolutely no way she can harm people with her powers. What she *can* do, what she did do that day was heal us and save our lives. She's freaking amazing, you idiot."

For some reason, his heart leapt. He supposed he could hear the rest of what Claire had to say. "What else?"

"Yay! You believe!" she squealed.

"I wouldn't go that far. Just tell me what else you've learned."

"So many, many things," she teased. "Dude, your virginity for one."

"My virginity?" Avery asked, an image of Zellie topless, leaning over him smiling, the street light making her hair glow like burning embers, popped into his head.

"Uh huh. I knew you'd wanna know about that one. It seems you're the one to blame for triggering Zellie's visions."

"Oh, how is that?" He kicked the covers off his feet. He was sweating despite the air conditioning vent right above his bed.

"The visions are triggered by your one true love, the person you're meant to be with forever. And you, Avery, are Zellie's trigger." She sighed dramatically.

"Okay, but what does that have to do with my virginity?"

"Duh," Claire huffed, "it means you two are definitely going to do it, it's *predestined*."

Avery surprised himself and laughed. “Let me see if I understand what you’re saying. Mrs. Wells can talk to my dad who Zellie didn’t kill and I’m the idiot virgin that started this whole thing in the first place.”

“Yup.” Claire swore. “Someone’s coming. I’ll call you back when I can.”

Avery set the phone in its cradle and tried to resume staring at the ceiling, but all he could see was Zellie. Her green eyes, her soft skin, the way she looked at him when he was about to kiss her, they way she’d looked at him when he’d called her a stupid freak. Damn. He felt his body hum with the electricity she caused every time he touched her. Damn. He *was* an idiot.

I walked out onto the porch and sat down next to Claire. “Purse bagel?” I handed her half a blueberry bagel with cream cheese.

She took it. “Don’t mind if I do.”

“How’re your parents?”

“Fine. Busy.” She tore off a chunk of bagel with her teeth.

“Grandma’s going to teach me to see the future next. Wanna watch your best freak forever get trance-y?”

Claire frowned at me. “I wish you’d stop calling yourself a freak. He’s going to feel so bad when--”

“He’s not going to feel anything because he never wants to talk to me again.” I stood up. “Come back inside if you want.”

Upstairs, Aunt Hazel and Melody had already cracked the case.

“Friday, two days from now, they serve chicken and noodles at the First Unitarian Church in Southwest, from one to five.” Melody folded her arms across her chest. “I’m totally good at this.”

I hugged her. “Yes, you are. You rock.” I turned to Grandma. “So, Friday, you think I can figure out how to rewind by then?”

“Definitely, we’ll have to try a few more good alleys I know of.” She grinned.

“My only choice is drunk people? Really? Can’t I rewind Melody?”

Claire came into the room shutting the front door behind her. “You can practice on me if you want.”

I didn’t know if that was such a good idea. I was getting weird vibes from my BFF. “Are you sure? Is it safe, Grandma?” I said.

“Hey! What about my safety?” Melody slapped my shoulder.

“What? I was kinda kidding when I said I would practice on you. I didn’t know that you guys were actually an option.”

“It won’t hurt...although it’s not customary to practice on people we know.” Grandma shrugged. “You can give it a try.” She came over to stand next to me. “Claire, why don’t you...take your shoes off and we’ll see if Zellie can put them back on.”

Claire sat down on the couch. With exaggerated movement she slipped her silver ballet flats from her feet and put them on the floor.

I put my hand out, fingers spread. I felt like a total dork. I stared at her forehead, burrowing my thoughts into her brain. Reach out. Pick them up. I focused. Claire leaned forward, picked up the shoes. She crossed her right ankle over her left knee. I was *totally* good at this! Claire slid one shoe on. Slid one shoe on. Slid one shoe on.

"I think you've got her on repeat," Melody said.

I dropped my hand down. "Ugh. I suck!"

Claire came to. She looked at her feet. "Didn't work, huh? Try again. It's like being on laughing gas at the dentist, no biggie." She took both of her shoes off again and placed them next to her on the couch.

"I want to try something." I'd been thinking a lot about The Rewind while I was falling asleep the night before. It wasn't my favorite thing to think about, but if this ability was going to help anyone, I needed to pull out all the stops. I stood in front of Claire. "I maybe have a theory." I put my arm out, aimed it. "Now, talk to me about Avery. I think I need to be emotional to rewind."

Claire grimaced. "Okay...so...I think you need to call him and let him know that saying you're a freak was a lame move. You need to tell him that he is going to damn well talk to you and he better thank his lucky stars that he's alive--"

Nothing. Wrong again. "It's not working. I don't want to say any of that stuff to him." I started to put my hand down.

"Wait," Claire said. "Pretend you're in church, or sitting behind him in school. I've watched you staring at the back of his head for years, Zellie. You love him and he loved you too. Don't forget that. Think about why you were..."

I saw him lean into me, rest his forehead on mine, heard him say, "I'm going to kiss you now." I felt his soft lips, ached for his fingertips pressing into the small of my back. Thigh touching thigh. My hands in his hair, sliding it through my fingers. His smell. His taste.

Claire froze for a second, and then she reached out and picked her shoes up off the couch.

"That's the key, Zellie," Grandma said.

Putting on the right shoe, followed by the left, Claire looked straight ahead and placed both feet on the floor.

"Figures. Whatever, he's still a buttwipe," Melody said as she went into the kitchen.

I brought my hand down. Between getting up earlier than normal, the excitement of the day, and all of the rewinding, I could feel exhaustion coming on. I went over to the couch and collapsed next to Claire. "Phew! I don't feel like I'm going to faint or anything, but I could use a nap."

Melody came back into the room and handed me a large glass of water.

"I think we've made some great progress today, don't you, Rachel?" Aunt Hazel said.

"I think my granddaughters did wonderfully...and Claire too of course."

"I've got several errands to run." Aunt Hazel went to the coat rack by the front door and retrieved her massive black purse. She put her sunglasses on. "Melody, you're welcome to tag along if you'd like."

"Sure, why not?" Melody followed Aunt Hazel out the door, turning to wave as she left. "See you all later."

"Bye." We all waved back.

Grandma pulled me up from the couch. "Let's get this turned back into a bed and let you rest." Claire helped her unfold it.

I fell onto the bed and snuggled with my pillow. I was so sleepy. Damn it, Avery, my trigger, my key. He'd better apologize and fall madly in love with me again; it was for the greater good, really. I needed him whether he knew it or not.

It was dinner time before I woke up. Aunt Hazel had ordered a pizza. She'd been too busy running errands to make anything from scratch like she normally did, which made her a way more normal person in my eyes. My mouth watered, I was star-to-the-ving. I grabbed a slice of pepperoni and perched on a kitchen chair, my legs tucked up to my chest.

"Want a pop, Zel?" Claire asked, taking a Coke from the fridge.

"Yes, please." I took the can. "How are you feeling? I'm still kinda wiped." I chugged half the pop.

"I'm good. You're the one that exerted all the energy." Claire sat down at the table, flopping two slices of pizza onto her paper plate and salting them.

"You'll get used to it eventually," Aunt Hazel said. "With Rachel it took about a month before she acclimated." She leaned back against the kitchen counter. She folded her pizza slice in half before she took a bite.

Grandma and Melody mopped the grease from their slices with napkins. We all ate. Claire's cell phone rang in her pocket. She took it out and flipped it open.

"It's my mom, I better take this." She dropped her pizza onto her plate and hurried out the front door.

Grandma raised one eyebrow, looking after her. That was strange. Maybe she was getting weird vibes from Claire too.

"Twice in one day?" Melody snorted. "I don't think they even talk to each other that much when they're in the same town. Wonder when our parents are going to call?"

I stretched my legs out in front of me and looked at Grandma. "Well, I was thinking that I might try and see what they're up to dream-wise?"

She nodded. "That would be okay. It really is the easiest of the abilities to get the hang of. All you have to do is picture the person and concentrate."

Melody took another piece of pizza from the box, she bypassed the grease mopping this time. "That's great, but I would actually like to hear their voices. Can we at least call Dad tomorrow?"

"We'll see, Melody." Aunt Hazel brushed crumbs from her hands into the sink. "Your grandma wants the timing to be just right with your mother. She doesn't want to hurt her anymore than she already has. We also don't want to risk your dad asking too many questions too soon or any of us giving too much away."

Melody crossed her arms across her chest. "Fine."

Grandma got up from the table and threw her paper plate away. She rinsed her pop can and tossed it into the recycling bin under the sink. "Who's up for some more *Big Brother*? I do hope they get rid of that girl with the impossibly fake breasts, they're so distracting."

Chapter Twelve

"Cool, Claire, thanks. I'll call you tomorrow and tell you what happened. Wish me luck." Avery hung up the phone and went down the hall to the guest bedroom. He knocked on the door. "Mrs. Wells?" She was crying. She was always crying.

"What is it, honey?" She blew her nose.

"I've...I just got off the phone with Claire. She's been telling me all sorts of interesting..." He looked down at the list in his hand, a list full of impossible things. "Can I come in? I've got something to show you." He tried the knob. It was locked.

"Hold on, I'll be right there." She shuffled to the door and opened it.

Mrs. Wells was wearing sweatpants and one of his dad's old t-shirts. Her eyes and nose were red and raw. She'd been staying with him since Zellie and Melody went to Portland. She said it was because he shouldn't be alone, and that it was just until his mom came back, whenever that was going to be. Avery knew it had something to do with Pastor Paul not liking the way she was carrying on about his dad.

Hell, even he was starting to feel better and the last time he'd talked to his dad they'd fought. Mrs. Wells was a wreck. It would be great if she *could* talk to his dad. Maybe he'd tell her to take a shower and eat something. Go take a walk. Leave the guest bedroom.

Avery handed her the list. "Like I said, I've been talking to Claire and there are some things you should know."

She scanned the list and handed it back to him. "Avery, honey," she said and her eyes filled with tears anew, "I would love nothing more than to see your dad again, but I think I know more about these abilities than Claire does." She tried to shut the door, but Avery stuck his foot in the doorway, holding it open.

"Try, for me. Please? If you can see him and I hold you hand, I can see him too." He'd be damned if he was going to let her give up that easily.

She stepped back and opened the door. They stood there for a moment and then sat on the end of the bed. She looked at him. She blushed the same way Zellie did. A pang of regret hit him. He was the stupid freak.

"All I'm supposed to do is think about your dad and if he's here I'll be able to see him?"

"That's what Claire said."

"If it was that easy, don't you think I would've felt him around me or something? Don't get your hopes up, okay? I doubt this is going to work." Mrs. Wells reclined on the bed and closed her eyes.

A minute later she sat up and grabbed Avery's hand, squeezing her eyes closed tight and then opening them up again. "Do you see him?"

Avery gripped her hand to keep them both from trembling. "Yeah, I see him." His dad was standing right in front of him. He looked different, sort of transparent? Yet he had the same clothes, same complexion, he didn't look dead...he looked peaceful. "Hi, Dad."

"Hi, Son, how's it going?"

"Uh, it's going weird." Still holding hands, Avery and Mrs. Wells scooted over, making room for him to sit down. "Where are you? In heaven? Purgatory? He--"

"Hey now!" his dad chuckled, sitting down on the bed. His weight didn't register. He put a hand on Mrs. Wells knee. "I've been with her since I died. I think this confirms that I'm officially attached to you, Gracie."

She tried to touch his hand, but hers passed through his and rested on her own knee. She left it there anyway. "You've been with me this whole time? Through everything?"

He nodded. He put his hand to her stomach and gazed into her eyes. "Everything."

Avery looked away, his dad's comment registering. He dropped Mrs. Wells hand. "I'll leave you guys alone for awhile." He got up and went into the hall, closing the door behind him. He leaned against it, listening in on their one-sided conversation.

"Yours, Mike," she said. "Of course I'm going to keep it!" She paused. "I know. Paul and Becky will be devastated, not to mention the kids." There was silence and then laughing. "You should've died a long time ago. It's the best thing that ever happened to us."

Avery slumped to the floor and crawled across the hall into the bathroom. He made it to the toilet and threw up. The best thing that had ever happened to Mrs. Wells and his dad was ruining his life. Didn't they see that? How could they be so selfish? How could his dad continue to torment his mom from beyond the grave? Another wave of nausea hit, he heaved again.

In the guest bedroom, Mrs. Wells giggled, oblivious, and said, "This is some crazy stuff, huh?"

Grabbing a wad of toilet paper, Avery wiped his mouth. He'd bought into Mrs. Wells theories and rules because Zellie had frightened him, because she had kept information from him. He could see now why she'd done that. Zellie was protecting him, keeping it together for the both of them. She was making sure they didn't become the next Mike and Gracie. And he'd treated Zellie like crap. Well, at least she'd thrown rocks at him. He would always have that precious memory.

Steadying himself against the wall, Avery stood and stumbled back across the hall. When he opened the door, Mrs. Wells had a goofy grin on her face.

He went to them, taking her hand and addressing them both. "I'm going over to Jason's for a few hours. Tomorrow I'm calling Zellie and begging her to come home. That is if she'll talk to me after what I've, we've, put her through."

"Son, it's still not a good idea--" his dad reached out to him.

Avery stepped back from him as his hand flowed through his shoulder. "No. You two don't get to tell me what to do anymore. I'm happy you get to be together, but maybe you should have taken that chance all those years ago, y'know?"

His dad and Mrs. Wells looked at him, confused. They were in their own world. "Because you're about to screw up all of our lives? Again? Forget it."

His dad reached out to him again. Avery stayed put this time. "No. You don't get to tell me what to do anymore, either of you. Zellie and I? We're going to do what we want. We're going to be together now, if she'll have me." Avery turned and left the room calling over his shoulder, "Mom and Pastor Paul better know about this baby by the time I get back. Everything out in the open. That's the only way I see this working."

Free from his guilt and his dinner, Avery jumped into the pickup and headed to Jason's.

I turned off the television and lay back in bed. It was eleven. Grandma was asleep in a chair with her feet propped up on the end of the fold-out couch. So much for guidance. Melody lay still beside me, probably worn out from her day of sleuthing. Claire slept face down with a pillow over her head. Aunt Hazel had gone into her bedroom hours ago.

For all intents and purposes I was alone. Just me and my half-assed psychic powers. All I had to do was give myself over to it. Apparently, my body knew how to use all of my abilities if I could just manage to get out of my own way.

I pictured my parents sleeping, dreaming away in their cozy little bedroom in Rosedell, a light summer quilt covering them. Dad was most likely snoring, his arms flung up above him. I imagined Mom, curled up on her side, her hair fanned out on the pillow. Content? I hoped they were. I closed my eyes. Put myself in their room, next to them, watching. The image crumbled and fell away.

Standing behind the pulpit, Dad spoke to the congregation. I looked out at them. Mom and Mr. Adams sat together in one pew. Melody and dream me, Claire, Avery, and Mrs. Adams sat in another. Dad held the Bible up over his head, the light through the stained glass windows illuminating the gold cross on its cover. We all snickered at him, holding our hands up to our mouths. Mom stood up and pointed at him, laughing the loudest. Dad threw the Bible. It hovered in the space above them and then burst into flames.

I opened my eyes. This was not helpful. Why wasn't Mom asleep? Was she conscious of Dad's nightmare? On the verge of coaxing him awake, soothing him?

Closing my eyes again, I turned onto my side. Of course I wasn't sleepy now. Should I try Avery? Risk knowing what was going on in his subconscious? With him, it somehow felt like a violation of his privacy but...so tempting. I better not. He'd be in my dreams soon enough when his vision made its nightly appearance.

I searched for the remote amongst the covers and turned the television back on, quickly turning the volume down. I ran through the channels until I found an infomercial. Those were good to fall asleep by.

"Hello, Avery." A female voice he didn't recognize said into the phone.

"Claire?" He looked at the clock on his bedside table. 7:12, why the hell did she keep calling so early? "Are you under a bed again? You sound different."

"No. This is Zellie's grandma," the voice whispered. "Listen closely. You cannot continue to be in touch with Claire or try to contact Zellie in any way. They will be back in Rosedell soon enough--"

"Zellie's grandma that's dead? As in Mrs. Wells' mom?"

"Yes, Avery, now pay attention. It is important that you don't call anymore."

Well, in that case, he'd just hop in the truck and drive up--

She sighed, annoyed. "Or come to Portland. This is altering your and Zellie's future in an unfavorable way. Her vision about you is changing. I've seen it."

Avery huffed. "Great. I'm supposed to believe you now? What is it with all of you grown-ups?"

Zellie's grandma huffed back. "There is nothing "with me" young man. If you want to survive another year on this earth you'll listen to me. No more calls. Got it? And not a word to Grace about me. We'll be in Rosedell on Monday." She hung up.

Screw that, Avery was sick of listening to adults, they didn't know what was going on any more than he did. He got out of bed and pulled his pajama pants on. Everything out in the open, no secrets. He crossed the hall to the guest bedroom and brought his hand up to knock on the door, when he heard Mrs. Wells talking to herself again.

Chapter Thirteen

I opened my eyes and looked toward the chair grandma had been sleeping in. I heard her talking in the other room but couldn't make out what she was saying. What the hell time was it anyway? I pawed at the end table next to the couch where Claire usually kept her phone, but it wasn't there. Must have fallen on the floor. Well, whatever time it was, I was awake, might as well try the dream thing with Mom--

My eyes snapped shut. Guess it was glimpse time again.

Mom rolled over in a strange bed and said, "I don't know how long it's going to take before I believe that you're actually here."

A transparent Mr. Adams grinned. He lay beside her. "We have forever, Gracie."

She snuggled into the pillow and glanced through him at the bedside table. There was a folded up piece of paper on it. "Can I try something?"

"Sure," he said.

She reached out, leaning into him. She inhaled sharply. "It feels like being in the static on the TV." She stayed there for a moment. "It's amazing." Electricity coursed through her veins.

He curved away from her. "We don't know what that'll do to you."

She pouted. "Fine, but it's not like I can say 'hand me that piece of paper.' I just wanted to try." She reached over him and retrieved it.

They lay on their backs, my mom reading aloud.

"One. Mrs. Wells can talk to Dad if she just concentrates." She motioned like she had a pen. "Check. Two. Her and Zellie can see other people's dreams." She turned her head to Mr. Adams, "I stumbled on that one on my own." She read the next item. "Three. They can see glimpses of the future. The big picture. If they focus on a specific event."

She flopped onto her side, facing Mr. Adams. "Jesus, just think of what I could've seen if I'd known that." She looked toward the ceiling. "Thanks, Mom!"

Both of their eyes opened wide. He grabbed her hand as best he could.

"Do you think?" Mom said, "Oh my God, what if they're both here? What if my parents have been with me all along?" Her eyes filled with tears. She rolled onto her back and shut her eyes. Tears spilled onto the bedspread. "Don't go anywhere, okay?"

"I'm staying put." He tried to squeeze her hand.

After a minute Mr. Adams cleared his throat. "Open your eyes, Gracie. Your dad's here."

"Daddy?" Another transparent man, tall, with dark brown hair, about the same age as my dad, stood next to Mom's bedside.

"Hey Red, it's been awhile."

Mom sat up and wiped her eyes with the back of her hand. "Is Mom with you?" She looked around the room.

Her dad reached out to her, cupped her face in his hands. "Oh, sweetie, your mom's not dead. She's in Portland."

She jumped up from the bed, rushing through her dad. "What? What are you talking about? Maybe you're confused."

"No, honey, I've been with her since I died. She can't see me like you can, but she knows I'm there. Now we can all be together again. I've been waiting so long."

Mom slid down the wall and slumped to the floor. She looked up at her dad. "She's in Portland? Where? With Aunt Hazel?"

"Yes, she's with Hazel and--"

"That's how Claire knew about all of this? Mom is with the girls?" She crawled to the dresser and picked up the phone.

I could hear the dial tone, like I was the one on the phone. This would be so cool if I could do it on purpose, instead of being forced to see things I didn't want to. Mom dialed.

"Hello?" Aunt Hazel answered.

"Hey, it's Grace. How are you? I'm doing great. Just sitting here with Dad and Mike Adams, havin' a chat. Can I talk to my mom? I hear she's not dead."

"Oh, dear." Aunt Hazel set the phone down with a thud.

Someone picked up the phone. Me and Mom could hear them breathing into it. "Mom? If it's you, if you're there, just...what the hell, Mom?"

"Grace, I can't begin to explain..." Grandma said, "Why can no one...Avery wasn't supposed to say anything until I could see you face to face."

"Avery didn't tell me, Dad did."

"Your father's there with you? Ugh! He wasn't supposed to say anything either. The last time I saw him--"

"So, you guys see each other from time to time?" She shot a look at her dad. He bowed his head.

"Yes, a few of the other seers I know can do what you can, so we talk when we get the chance."

Mom's face flushed. "Were you ever going to tell me, come see me?"

Grandma sighed. "Monday, honey. We're all coming back to Rosedell on Monday. We'll sort it out. Zellie has a rewind to do tomorrow, and then we'll tie up some loose ends and be on our way. Can you please wait until then?"

Mom hung up the phone. She shut her eyes tight. When she opened them again, transparent Grandpa was gone.

Mr. Adams went to her, his arms outstretched. "It's going to be okay. There were bound to be difficult moments and you've had most of them within the last twenty-four hours. Come here." He put his arms around her, pushing his chest into her face. "Get a little static."

"My mom is going to be here on Monday."

"We'll deal with it then." He backed away from her. She shivered. "Hey, you want to go to the cabin for the weekend?"

"What about Avery?" Mom said.

"He'll be fine for a few days. Probably enjoy the alone time. C'mon, Zellie's not in town. We'll leave him a note." He winked at her.

She winked back.

My eyes jolted open and I fought the urge to barf, then the phone rang. I heard Aunt Hazel answer it in her bedroom and say, "Oh, dear."

Melody put the phone on speaker so that we could both talk to Dad. The answering machine picked up. "You've reached the Wells family!" he said in a sing song voice. Then we all said our names individually. "Paul. Grace.

Zellie. And Melody! Leave a massage at the beep!" Melody cringed at the massage part. I giggled remembering she'd thought that was really funny at the time. Beeeeeeeep. "Uh, hey Dad," Melody said, "Please call us at Aunt Hazel's as soon as you get this. We really need to talk to you. Love you, Daddy."

"Love you, Dad," I chimed in before I realized that he probably didn't want to hear from me.

Mel hung up the phone and flopped down on the couch next to Claire. I sat on the other side. We listened as Aunt Hazel and Grandma argued in hushed tones in the bedroom.

Claire scooted down into the couch until her butt was almost off the edge. She put a throw pillow over her face. "Smother me, Zel. Your grandma is going to put some sort of voodoo curse on me. Please have mercy on my soul."

I took the pillow and tossed it on the floor. "She's not going to curse you. I don't even think that's one of our abilities. She's just mad, but whatever, it's not like she hasn't majorly screwed things up. My mom would have freaked out anyway."

We'd all heard Grandma talking on the phone to Mom that morning, it was kinda hard not to. Aunt Hazel had stormed into the kitchen leaving her bedroom door open and muttering to herself, "this is what happens when Retro's try to do a Lookout's job." Caught off guard for once, Grandma had her back to the door and didn't know we were listening in.

When Aunt Hazel came into the family room carrying a pot of tea and mugs, I realized she was going to try and be comforting, so I took pity on her. I told her and Mel and Claire everything I'd seen and heard in my glimpse, but was vague about the way Mom and Mr. Adams had acted with each other. I had no idea what I was going to do with that information, if I should tell Dad or force Mom to or wait and see what happened. Which, thanks to my inability to master my abilities, it wasn't likely that I would be able to see what would happen until about a minute before it did. Super helpful.

After I'd spilled my news, Aunt Hazel seemed even more mad at Grandma, who, when she had eventually figured out we'd heard her talking to Mom, had shut the bedroom door and not come out.

Determined to have all the facts, Aunt Hazel had gone in to confront Grandma almost an hour ago. An hour of hushed arguing between them and one of anticipatory torture for Claire.

"What are they talking about in there?" Claire slid all the way to the floor and beat herself over the head with the pillow. "I just wanted everything with you and Avery to be okay."

I sank to the floor and lay next to her. "I know. What all did you tell him anyway?" I was not going to allow myself even a sliver of hope. Yet. I simply wanted to check what she said against the list Mom had read in my glimpse. Yeah right.

"Not that much, nothing about your grandma, just that you didn't kill his dad."

I gave her a knowing look.

"That's all, I swear!" Claire thought for a second, "Well, okay, and also the dream thing and the glimpse thing."

Melody reached over and threw the pillow down the hall. "Hey! You've got a nickname after all, how about The Meddler?"

"Shut up." I kicked her in the shin. Claire was just being Claire and she couldn't help when things turned out Claire-y.

"Whatever!" Melody said.

"He was okay with all of these things? He didn't freak out? Because the Avery I left behind should have definitely freaked out." The Avery I left behind should have hung up on Claire the second he heard her voice.

"I finessed him a little. I may have mentioned his virginity," she said.

I threw my arms over my eyes. Not that again. "You didn't."

Grandma and Aunt Hazel came out into the family room. Aunt Hazel spoke. "Well girls, apparently your grandma has had a glimpse that she forgot to mention to us, so it looks like we're all going to Rosedell on Monday."

She glared at Grandma. "Although, we usually need more than two days to wrap up a case after a rewind, especially when it involves a new Retroact, but Rachel thinks it will all be fine, because she's seen it. Well, bully for her!" Aunt Hazel went into the kitchen and put the kettle on to boil, again.

"Have you called your father?" Grandma asked, attempting to look like she wasn't in trouble.

"Yeah, he wasn't there," Melody said. "I left a message."

"Okay. Keep trying." She handed Melody her cell phone. "I'd like to set up a meeting with everyone at your house."

"Yeah, we know." Melody said, giving Grandma her best disappointed Aunt Hazel look. She *was* learning from the master.

"Zellie, could you come here please?" I got up off the floor and went to her. "I'm sorry I kept this from you. I was only trying to keep you focused on your rewind." Grandma grasped my hand, transferring the glimpse.

Everyone was at our house. Dad and Avery sat on the couch, both smiling at me, reassuring. Mom was in her chair. She didn't look so good, like maybe she was sick to her stomach. The rest of the glimpse played out.

I looked at Grandma. "I hope it really goes like that. I wish it was one hundred percent."

She hugged me. "Let's get in gear for tomorrow. We'll worry about Monday on Monday." She nodded toward the door. "Let's go to Voodoo Doughnut and get some breakfast, give your old Aunt Hazel some time to herself."

As we headed out the door, Aunt Hazel called from the kitchen, "Bring me a Cap'n Crunch if they have any."

Grandma grinned. "Sure, Sis."

Chapter Fourteen

At 12:30 on Friday afternoon Melody, Aunt Hazel, Grandma and I got into the Beemer. Claire had orders to stay in the apartment and wait for Dad to call.

Once we were within four blocks of the Unitarian church, Grandma parked the car. Aunt Hazel took a couple of ball caps out of a Goodwill bag and handed them to me and Grandma. “These might make you look less conspicuous.”

“Thanks.” I threaded my ponytail through the back of my hat.

Grandma offered hers to Melody. “I’ll look more conspicuous with this on than not. You can wear it if you like.”

“You sure? Your hair’s pretty noticeable with the gray stripes.” Melody checked with Aunt Hazel and then put the hat on backwards and to the right. “Let’s roll.”

We walked the four blocks to the church and then went around to the side where a line was forming. I kept my head tilted down, scoping out the group as best I could. There was no sign of David or his attacker yet.

Up near the front of the line I noticed a blonde boy about my age, maybe a little older, with a man that was probably his dad. The boy had a pleasant expression on his face, but the circles under his eyes were dark.

I wondered where he slept. Maybe at a shelter? Most likely in a park. It was too bad he was going through such hard times. I considered all the people in the line and felt awful that they were there, that there even needed to be a soup kitchen. But this guy, I don’t know, he was good looking. Way too good looking. He was out of place. I was getting such a weird vibe from him that I didn't even feel guilty about noticing his hotness. Not that I didn't have free reign to check out other guys or anything, but, well, I might be letting myself have a glimmer of hope after what Grandma saw.

I smelled David before I saw him. A few people behind me, he reeked of whiskey and pine. I tried to keep it together. No need for a vision right now. My mission was clear. I made eye contact with my family. They all nodded in recognition.

From the front of the line, I felt another set of eyes on me. The blonde boy. Was he checking me out? I dared a glance in his direction. Hmm, it seemed more like he was trying to figure me out. He smiled. I leaned toward Mel and whispered, "Hottie at twelve o'clock."

Melody pretended to stretch her neck, twisting it from side to side. "Yum. Someone's pretty hot for a homeless dude," she whispered back through her teeth.

"Girls," Grandma hissed. "Zellie, I believe you need to be thinking about Avery. Melody...just stop."

The doors to the church opened and the line moved forward. "Here we go," Aunt Hazel said.

We entered the gymnasium from the side. To our left were cafeteria tables laid out in six rows seven tables deep. The food tables were set up underneath the basketball hoop at the far end.

Volunteers wearing hairnets and white aprons dished chicken and noodles out onto paper plates. There were also green salads in Styrofoam bowls and a large plastic bin of apples. The last table held two industrial size orange thermoses full of iced tea and lemonade. The line wound through the door, down the length of the basketball court.

As we neared the food, Grandma looked around and then slipped a twenty into the donation box at the beginning of the line. I'd put her up to it, I didn't think it was cool to take food away from people that really needed it. She'd kind of complained and blathered on about how we were supposed to be undercover saving lives, but whatevs, it appeared that she had listened to me anyway.

Each of us took a plate of noodles and a bowl of salad and then they all followed me to a table two rows in. We sat down, heads bowed, picking at our food. "If I'm right," I said, "David should sit three tables down."

He walked past us and sat three tables down. The pine burned my nose. Grandma grabbed my hand. "Hold on. Take a deep breath. I can go get you some tea."

"I'm okay." I looked around the room, studied the line. "I don't see the other guy yet, do you?"

Grandma scanned the room guardedly. "He just walked in. Get ready everyone. This is going to happen fast."

I counted to ten and then stood up from the table, my plate of food in hand. I paced myself, not wanting to get to David before anything happened. The plan was to drop my plate near him and conduct the rewind from the floor. It would be more discreet that way.

I noticed the blonde boy stand up and start walking toward me. This was not a good time to chat me up dude! Who was I kidding, he was at least three levels hotter than I was, and he was probably going to get some lemonade.

I concentrated on thoughts of Avery. He leaned in. I'm going to kiss you now. Electricity. My hands in his hair. I was a table length and a half away.

The attacker shouted from the food line, "Hey! David! David?" I watched him duck his head down. Avery brushing his cheek against mine. Tucking my hair behind my ear.

"Hey. David. You going to pretend you don't know me?" He stumbled towards David, dragging his left foot.

David turned away from his plate and looked over his shoulder.

I glared at the attacker and ran right into the blonde boy coming up the aisle. We both dropped our plates and stooped down to feign cleaning them up.

The attacker pulled the knife from his jeans pocket. I shot my right hand out in front of me, over the blonde boy's left shoulder, my fingers spread. I was going to have to worry about what to tell him later. Or not. He cocked his wrist backwards over his right shoulder, spreading his fingers wide.

As the attacker moved forward, sticking the tip of the knife in David's neck, he froze. I didn't know if I was freezing him or if...who was this guy? We backed the attacker away, holding the knife in between him and David for a split second. Blondie apparently found the whole thing amusing. He winked at me.

"I got this," he said.

I put my hand down, shocked. The nerve of him! Talk about majorly stealing my thunder! He was doing the rewind without even looking.

He twirled the knife around with one hand, making it do figure eights, while he held the attacker suspended with the other.

"Benjamin." Blondie's father said from behind him. "That's enough. The cops are walking in the door."

Faltering for a moment at the sound of his name, Benjamin recovered, swiftly returning the knife to the attacker's hand. The whole thing only lasted about twenty seconds. He winked at me again and swiped two fingers under his eyes, smudging the dark circles. "I'm method," he joked. Then he stood up and followed his father out the door that led to the sanctuary.

Four police officers rushed into the gym from the street.

On cue, Melody screamed, "He's got a knife!"

Everyone backed away, except me; I remained stooped over in a daze. What the hell just happened? Grandma grabbed me under the arm and pulled me up out of the way, just as the police got to the scene. Melody stepped forward, pointing to the attacker, who was now just a very stunned man.

Grandma walked me from the church to the car. We were to wait there while Melody made a statement to the police. Aunt Hazel was supervising her.

I ripped my hat from my head the second I climbed into the backseat of the Beemer. I was sweating buckets, my heart racing. "Who were those men? I thought all the Retroacts you knew were women?"

Grandma shook her head in disbelief. "They are." She turned to me. "I have absolutely no knowledge of any male Retroacts. Some seers, but they're few and far between. There are no men in The Society. We've never had a call for them." She rummaged around in her purse until she found her cell phone. She dialed. "Hello? Candace? It's Rachel. You would not believe what just happened to my granddaughter."

She listened.

"So you glimpsed it? What'd you see? Yes, her first intentional rewind and it was hijacked by a male Retroact. A boy! Have you ever encountered such a thing?"

She listened again.

"Benjamin. He was with his father I'm guessing. I'll send Hazel down at once. I've got a prior engagement here. No, it can't wait. I'll come right after. Tuesday, Wednesday at the latest. Bye. See you then." She flipped the phone shut and threw it in her purse.

We sat in the car waiting in silence. Grandma was super pissed off. I sunk down in the back seat and drank two bottles of water out of the six-pack Melody had brought for me.

Aunt Hazel appeared at the passenger side window and flung open the door. "I'm to go straight to Los Angeles, I assume?"

Grandma put the key in the ignition. "You are."

Melody hopped into the backseat and yanked her seatbelt on. "Well, your part sucked, but I totally rocked it again."

I did not respond. I stared out the window, searching for Benjamin among the crowds on the sidewalk. I'm method. What the hell did that mean? The way he'd twirled that knife. Cocky, like he'd been rewinding for years. Was he going to be there every time? Had he had the vision himself or just seen it in my head? In *my* head.

No one spoke until we were crossing the Burnside Bridge. Aunt Hazel turned to me. "Were you two rewinding in tandem?"

I shrugged. "It seemed easier than before, so maybe he was doing all the work, but I'm still really dehydrated and hot like I've been rewinding."

"Hmm, and you were thinking about Avery?"

"Yes, all the way to the table. Although I stopped when he, Benjamin, walked into me."

"Interesting," Aunt Hazel said. "I suppose the older man was his Lookout. What an odd pair." She turned and faced front.

"I don't get what the big deal is. So, there were two Retroacts on one case? Double the rescue power," Melody said.

Grandma slowed for a stoplight. "The big deal is that two Retroacts never have the same vision. Either it was a fluke, a glitch in the supernatural system, or this Benjamin somehow got into Zellie's head without knowing her." The light turned green. "The scary thing is that he wasn't careful. Twenty seconds is a long time when someone's twirling a knife in the air in front of a bunch of bystanders. He put us all in danger. He could potentially jeopardize The Society and start a modern day witch hunt."

"Oh," Melody took my hand, "that is a big deal."

Grandma parked the Beemer in front of The Haven and we all got out except for her. "I'll just be a minute," Aunt Hazel said.

Once inside the apartment she went straight to her bedroom and came out wheeling a suitcase behind her. She gave each of us a quick peck on the cheek. "It's been great having you girls stay with me. You're welcome anytime. Give your mother my love." Then she was out the door, thumping her suitcase down the stairs.

Claire looked up from the couch. "Where's she going? Is everything all right?"

I filled her in on Benjamin.

"Method as in method actor?" Claire snorted. "That's pretentious."

“Totally,” I agreed.

“Whatever, you thought he was hot.” Melody kicked off her shoes and sat on the floor, leaning back against the television table.

“Oh really?” Claire reached over the back of the couch and dragged me around to sit next to her. “Hotter than Avery?”

I blushed. “Different than Avery, he had highlights, like a movie star or something. He just looked too...well groomed to be in a soup line.”

“Oh.” Claire giggled. “I get it.”

“I don’t. Care to share your insights?”

“He’s totally gay, Zel. Highlights, knows acting terms, kinda bitchy, hotter than your average boy? I suppose he could be metro, but my gaydar’s pretty good.”

“What?” I thought for a moment. “Well, that does sort of make sense. Grandma said she’d never heard of a male Retroact, but if he’s gay...I mean, the whole thing’s triggered by attraction.” Okay, so I maybe pictured Avery and Benjamin wrestling shirtless in the middle of a soccer field, but just for a little bit.

“That must have been some coming out. ‘Hey Dad, I’m gay and also have visions of when people are gonna die. Glad we had this talk.’” Claire shook her head. “Bummer.”

“I don’t know, he seemed pretty pleased with the whole situation. I did not get the sense that he was bummed at all.”

Melody sat up straighter. “Okay, gay or not, he’s still a threat to you and The Society. I say we tell Grandma that we want to go home tomorrow.” She looked to Claire. “Did Dad call? I bet he would be happy if we came back early.”

"Yeah, I talked to him about half an hour ago. He told me like a billion times that he'd do whatever you guys needed him to. He's going to call Avery this afternoon." She gave me a reassuring smile.

"What if he hasn't had enough time to set up the meeting?" I thought of Mom and Mr. Adams at the cabin. I still hadn't decided if I should be the one to tell my dad that Mom was cheating on him with the spirit of Mr. Adams, or wait and let the situation take care of itself. All this Benjamin business was not helping me live in denial. "I don't know if we should deviate from the plan."

"Forget the plan. We have to get out of town." Melody rolled her eyes. "Again."

"Fine, call Dad." There was no stopping Melody when she wanted her way, a personality trait that served her well as a Lookout and made her way more annoying as a little sister. I was just going to have to think on my feet and hope for the best. Because that strategy had worked out so well for me in the past. Ha.

"I'll check the vision Grandma had and see if anything changes too much. Then I'll try and get a glimpse of my own." I turned to Claire. "You better start packing now, your shoes alone are going to take an hour."

She saluted. "I'm on it. Guess I should call my parents and tell them that I'm coming home. Have you seen my phone? I can't find it anywhere."

I lay back on the couch and closed my eyes. "Sorry, I haven't. Just use the cordless after Melody's done with it. Aunt Hazel won't care if you make one phone call."

While Mel and I busied ourselves, Claire got down on her hands and knees and started pulling shoes out from underneath the furniture.

Avery was enjoying his four o'clock bowl of cereal at the kitchen table wearing only his boxer shorts when the phone rang. He chewed quickly and swallowed before answering.

"Hello?"

"Hey," Claire whispered.

"Aw, crap. Man, I'm not supposed to talk to you. Zellie's grandma is going to kill me."

"You talked to Psychic Granny?"

"Yup. She tricked me by calling on your phone and told me not to talk to you anymore, not to contact Zellie and not to tell Mrs. Adams that she was alive. She's scary." He shivered.

"That Retro-bitch stole my phone!" Claire scoffed. "Well, her plan was a big fail. It's all out in the open now. Look, I thought I'd give you a heads up. Pastor Paul is going to call you shortly and ask you over for a meeting tomorrow. We're coming home early. You can be there, right?"

"Definitely. I'm prepared to do anything to get Zellie back now."

"Cool. That's what I wanted to hear. Okay, I better go-
-"

"Wait, is Mrs. Wells supposed to be at this meeting too?"

"Yeah, well it's at her house, so I'm guessing she'll be there," Claire said.

"Crap. Not if she's shacked up with my dead Dad at the family cabin she won't."

"What?"

"Yeah. Just because you guys left doesn't mean that the craziness left with you." Avery shook his head. "You said everything was out in the open, but it doesn't sound like you guys know what everything is."

"Spill. Now."

"Zellie's mom has been living with me since you all left for Portland. I thought it was because Pastor Paul didn't like it that she was so sad about my dad, but it's way worse than that, it's because she's pregnant with his baby."

"Holy tele-freaking-novella."

"And..."

"There's more?" Claire gasped.

"And," Avery began again, "because of our meddling, telling Mrs. Wells about her ability and everything, she and my dad are totally all over each other and lovey-dovey and super gross."

"Yuck. So I guess Pastor Paul and Mrs. Wells are, what, gonna get a divorce?"

"Well, I don't know. I tried to threaten the lovebirds into telling my mom and Pastor Paul about the baby last night, but of course they didn't listen to me. I'm visiting Mom this evening, I guess I'll tell her then. You think I should break the news to Pastor Paul when he calls?"

Claire snorted. "I don't think you should have to be dealing with this at all. Stupid grown-ups." She thought for a second. "I know this is going to sound crazy, but why don't you invite Pastor Paul to go with you to visit your mom and then tell them together, that way if--"

"If my mom has another breakdown, you mean, then I can use Pastor Paul as a human shield."

"You know that is not what I meant. I was only thinking they might be comforting to each other because they're in kinda the same boat. That's all. Your mom is not going to have another breakdown, man. It will be okay."

"If you say so." The call waiting beeped on his phone. "I gotta go, Pastor Paul's calling."

"Okay, see you tomorrow. Try and get Mrs. Wells to the meeting if you can."

"Peace out."

"Peace."

I'd been lying on the couch with my eyes closed for half an hour, hoping to get my own glimpse of our homecoming, but I wasn't getting anything but blips from Grandma's glimpse. I opened my eyes and looked around the empty family room. Melody was making something to eat in the kitchen and Claire was outside talking to her parents on the phone. I was alone. I was relaxed. I was focused. Why wasn't the glimpse thing working? Maybe I was concentrating on the wrong event? So, no homecoming. What else did I want to see?

My eyes snapped shut. Body knows best.

The door to Mrs. Adams room was buzzed open. She didn't turn from the window as the doctor entered the room.

"Good afternoon, Becky. How are you feeling?" The doctor pulled the other of the two chairs in the room over to the window and sat next to her.

She sighed and looked at the doctor, gave her a weak smile. "Okay. I had a good group last night."

The doctor smiled back. "That's what Dr. Plett said." She flipped through the papers on her clipboard. "Since you're doing so well, how would you feel about having a visitor?"

"Who's going to visit me?" Mrs. Adams asked.

"It looks like we had a call this afternoon from..." She flipped through the papers again. "A Paul Wells? Ah, your pastor? He's here to see you now if you're up for it."

Mrs. Adams shrugged, looking disappointed. "That would be fine."

The doctor put a hand on her arm and gave it a gentle squeeze. "Let's go see your visitor then."

My dad set a small bouquet of red carnations on one of the black vinyl couches in the visitors lounge and took off his jacket. He laid it over the back of the couch and sat down, careful not to smush the flowers. The visitors lounge was empty except for one older lady in some dusty rose scrubs at the nurse's station.

The door buzzed and Mrs. Adams stepped into the lounge. She was wearing jeans and a teal t-shirt. She'd changed her clothes.

Dad stood, grabbed the flowers from the couch and thrust them out to her. "Hi Becky, thanks for seeing me. You look good."

She took the flowers from him, a puzzled look on her face. "Thanks." She sniffed at the flowers and then sat down. "Sit, please. It's nice to see a familiar face."

They sat for a moment in awkward silence.

"So, Avery's doing well," my dad finally said. "Grace has been staying with him at your house, didn't know if you knew that?"

She nodded.

He prattled on. "He's been to church...mostly hanging out with Jason Erickson, playing a bit of soccer. He seems to be adjusting to his...situation."

"That's great," Mrs. Adams said. "He could come see me now if he wanted to." She lowered her head. "I'm ready for that, if he wants to."

Dad reached out and patted her knee. "Actually, he wanted to come visit this evening, but, uh, something came up. Do you know when you'll be returning to Rosedell?"

She shook her head. "I'm not sure when I get to come home. Maybe September?" She looked into his eyes. "Can you spare Grace for that long? The girls are gone too aren't they?"

He chuckled. "Yes, I've been a man left to his own devices. The girls are coming home tomorrow though. As far as Grace...I've been doing fine without her. It's something I'll have to get used to."

"Oh." Mrs. Adams looked at the spot on her wrist where a watch would be and then around the room for a clock. "Well, it's been nice to see you--"

"Um, wait Becky, this isn't just a social call." Dad took a deep breath and then blew the air slowly out through his nose. "I have something to tell you, bad news for you, for me too, really." He took another deep breath and then squared his shoulders. "I paid Grace a visit before I came over here. Actually Grace and Mike--"

"That's not funny, Paul." Mrs. Adams stood up and looked around, flustered.

Dad stood and put a hand on her shoulder. "No. It's not *funny and I'm* not *kidding." He paused. "I don't know what you remember, or what you believe to be true...about the accident?"*

"Are you telling me Mike's not dead?"

"No, he is. Do you remember the thing that Zellie did? And you knew about Grace? That all really happened. We all were a part of it."

She broke from his grasp and started pacing. "Okay. Yeah. I know, I mean I remember kind of. What does this have to do with...more bad news?"

"As it turns out," Dad sat on the edge of the couch, leaning forward and resting his elbows on his knees, "Grace has the ability to communicate with the dead. If you hold hands with her, he's...Mike's standing right there." Dad raked his hands through his hair.

"And they're what, together now?" Her voice rose.

He nodded his head. "Apparently. On the day of the accident they slept together and Grace is pregnant."

Mrs. Adams turned to him, staring, her mouth agape. She plopped down next to him on the couch. "I'm sure they have a room here for you if you'd like."

He cringed. "Do you think there's a support group for men whose wives left them for a ghost?"

"Those are some pretty narrow parameters." They looked at each other. Mrs. Adams burst out laughing. My dad joined in.

After a moment, nearly gasping for air, she managed to say, "Screw them. They freaking deserve each other."

He wiped his eyes. "That's really healthy of you Becky, I was considering vandalism."

"What? The truck? Be my guest. That was always their thing, had nothing to do with me." She exhaled, letting out the last few giggles.

"Avery's driving it now. I suppose I'll let it be." Dad smiled.

"His sixteenth birthday. He got his license?"

Dad patted her knee. "First try."

"Hey, why did you have to come tell me all of this?" Mrs. Adams asked.

"Well, when I talked to Avery this afternoon he told me about Grace and Mike and asked if I would come along with him to tell you. But something like this? It's not Avery's responsibility." Dad shrugged. "So, I went to talk to Grace and Mike and we all decided you'd react better hearing it from me, I guess. Grace didn't want to set you off."

Mrs. Adams snorted. "I bet she didn't." She turned to look at him.

He shook his head. "It's ridiculous, you should have seen them. They were so happy to be together that I don't think they even realized what it was going to do to us, to the kids." He clenched his jaw. "It just makes me furious. I trusted her and she what? Thought of me as good enough? A nice person? That my being a pastor would make me more understanding? Because it doesn't. If anything it's...goddamned embarrassing, that's what it is." He released Mrs. Adams from the tight grip he had on her knee. "Sorry, didn't mean to crush you."

"It's fine. Nice to know that you actually have some balls, Pastor Paul." She picked up her carnations and stood. "Want to join me for dinner? It's Salisbury steak."

"That would be great." He got up from the couch and grabbed his jacket. "Shall we drown our sorrows in gravy?"

"Amen." Mrs. Adams said.

My eyes shot open and I ran to the bathroom. This time I did barf.

Mom was going to have a *baby*? Great. So, now I didn't have to break the news to my dad that my mom was cheating on him with a ghost, I just had to tell Melody that she wasn't going to be the youngest anymore. I didn't know which was worse.

I wiped my face with a wet washcloth and looked in the mirror. My reflection made me burst into tears, I hadn't been aware of how worn out I looked. I shouldn't look like this; there shouldn't be bags under my eyes and creases in my forehead from worrying and keeping secrets. I was sixteen, not forty-six. I thought about what Dad had said about Avery*, it's not his responsibility*. Well, it wasn't mine either. Let the grown-ups sort their own messes out, all I wanted to concentrate on was getting my boyfriend back and tomorrow, God and glimpse willing, I would get my chance.

Chapter Fifteen

Rosedell looked different somehow. Smaller. Quieter. Maybe it was only through my eyes. I had changed so much, how could it have looked the same?

I twisted toward Claire and Melody in the backseat of the Beemer. "Does it look different here to you?"

Claire shrugged. "Not really."

Melody didn't bother looking up from her video game. "Nope."

I turned back around, staring out the front window. "Grandma, I'm nervous that things are not going to go the way that you saw them." I had tried to get another glimpse for myself, but all I'd conjured up was the family room with no one in it.

She reached over and took my hand. I closed my eyes and sped through her glimpse, pausing on Mom's reaction to seeing her mother in the flesh.

Grandma squeezed my hand. "You let me deal with Grace."

I paused ever so slightly on Avery's expression. I didn't really want Grandma seeing that. I let go of her hand.

She chuckled.

"Zel's thinking about Avery again, isn't she?" Claire chimed in.

Grandma nodded her head.

We drove through downtown, stopping every twenty feet for a crosswalk. Flyers for the upcoming rodeo hung in all of the storefronts except Adams Insurance. A lot of people were out.

In the summer Rosedell got plenty of tourists. They stayed out at the lodge, played golf, and came into town for local color, cheap t-shirts, and ice cream at the Hitchin'Post.

I grinned when the top scoop of vanilla slid off of a little girl's cone and plopped onto the sidewalk. As we stopped to let people cross the street, just to see if I could, I rewound it back in place. It worked. Already getting better the closer I got to Avery. The little girl looked confused for a second and then carried on eating her ice cream.

We all groaned when passing the school.

"I went there too, you know," Grandma said. "It hasn't changed at all."

"Sad, isn't it?" Melody quipped.

Grandma turned onto our street. Everyone took a deep breath. She pulled into the driveway and parked. We all got out. "You can get your bags later girls, I don't know about you, but I'm anxious to get this over with."

Melody went up the front steps first and opened the door.

Mom was sitting in her overstuffed green chair. Avery and Dad sat on opposite ends of the couch. Dad rushed to meet us as soon as Melody entered the room. He grabbed Melody and I and even Claire into a bear hug.

"I'm so glad you're back! I've missed you girls so much. I don't think we've ever been away from each other for this long." He held me at arms length to look at my face and then wrapped me in his arms again.

My heart felt like it was going to explode with happiness. My daddy loved me again! Maybe things were gonna go okay after all.

"We missed you too, Dad," Melody said, grabbing Grandma and pushing her towards him. "This is Grandma Rachel."

That settled him down. He shook her hand quickly and then gestured for her to go over to Mom. "I'm sure you two have a lot to catch up on."

Mom rose from her chair, tears visible in her eyes. Grandma reached out to her, cupping her face in her hands. "Hi, Gracie."

"Hi." Mom took her mother's hands from her face and held them in her own. The tears were coming at full force now. "I don't know if I can do this!" She ran from the room, Grandma hurried after her.

I looked away from them to Avery. He must be really uncomfortable witnessing all of this. But he wasn't. He was looking at me, a wistful smile on his face. My heart jumped a little. Okay, a lot.

Dad spoke up. "Zellie, how do you want to do this? You've got the room. I want to hear whatever you have to say, I think Avery does too."

I chewed at my bottom lip, deciding. "Um, why don't we sit down and I'll talk for a little bit. I know you guys have questions and I do have more answers for you than the last time we were all together." I checked with Avery, he seemed receptive. "I know you heard a lot of this from Claire, Avery, so stop me if I'm being redundant."

He nodded.

"Hopefully, whatever I can't clear up for you, Grandma can when she's done talking to Mom." I turned to Dad. "Thanks for bringing everyone together."

"It wasn't me honey, Avery got your mom to show up." He returned to his seat on the couch.

Claire and Melody leaned against the kitchen wall.

So far so good, pretty much as Grandma had seen it. I started in on the explaining. "Okay, here's the short version. Grandma is a seer and she belongs to a group of female seers called The Society. They're all over the world and there are thousands of them."

Avery nodded his head knowingly and Dad just sat there staring at me. I kept on. "The abilities are hereditary, obviously. Grandma is the first seer in our family as far as she knows. There are different abilities, not all of us seers are the same. Grandma is a Retroact and so am I-that means she can do that rewinding thing that I did."

It was quieter than church in here! I couldn't have felt more awkward. "So, Mom doesn't rewind, but she does have the ability to communicate--"

"I know, Zel," Avery said, "I've talked to my dad. It's...good?" He grinned.

"Oh! Great, got that out of the way." I glared at Claire. Would have been nice to know that. Here I'd been worried about keeping all of these secrets, but I was starting to get the feeling that all of the cats were already out of all of their damn bags. "Well, the last major thing is that I can't do harm with my abilities." I looked to Dad, surprised that he seemed shocked. I smiled great big. "I didn't hurt Mr. Adams."

He clapped his hands together. "Oh! That's wonderful. That is the best news I've had in a long time." He jumped to his feet and pulled me into another bear hug.

"So, what you're saying Zel is that you saved us all, some of us from death, and then we all treated you like crap?" Avery stated.

I teared up. Frickity frack Claire! She better never hold back from me again. "Yeah, that sounds right."

Avery rose from the couch and put a tentative hand to my face. "I'm so sorry Zellie...all of those horrible things I said to you." He brushed the tears from my cheek with his thumb. "Please forgive me. I'm a complete idiot. I mean, if you want to go out to the driveway, push me down and grind gravel into my eye sockets...I totally deserve it."

If I hadn't felt like I was taking a shower in Pine-Sol, I might have been worried by his public display of affection. "Forgiven," was all I could say before the vision overtook me.

I blinked hard and came to, not that surprised to find I was sitting on the couch. "Thanks, Avery," I smiled at him and took his hand.

Dad cleared his throat, eyeing our clasped hands. "This is all going to take a lot for me to get used to. My first concern is for you, Zellie." He took on his "I'm responsible for keeping your soul from burning in hell" tone. "I'm not sure that I want you acting on your visions or being in this society organization or rushing back into things with Avery."

I felt Avery's palms break out into a sweat. Mine weren't far behind.

"I have nothing against you son, but you broke my kid's heart. I'd like everyone to proceed with caution, okay?" Dad put a hand on my shoulder.

I let go of Avery's hand.

Mom and Grandma came back into the room. Mom's eyes were puffy and red, but she had a faint smile on her face. She extended her arms out to me. "Come here my sweet girl. I'm so sorry for how I treated you."

I got up from the couch and walked into her waiting arms. Love struck liar, or not, she was still my mom.

Melody harrumphed. “Does anyone have anything they wanna say to me? Anybody feel like giving me a hug?”

Mom and Dad and I descended on her, smothering her with hugs and kisses. Claire was caught in the crossfire, but did nothing to stop it.

“Grandma? Avery? Get your butts on over here!” I waved them into the group.

I put my arm around Avery’s waist, tears finding their way down my face once again. The electricity of our bond was still there despite our separation. I hoped we never had to endure being apart ever again.

On my other side, Dad leaned in and kissed the top of my head. I felt better knowing that he was scared for me and not scared of me anymore.

Mom hugged Melody and held onto Grandma’s hand, smiling more than she had in years. Claire and Avery shared a conspiratorial look and then broke out laughing.

Grandma hadn’t seen this part, this dysfunctional family group hug and I was glad. We were all happy in this moment. Yes, it was cheesy, and yes we all had so many things to work out and to get through, but in that moment I didn’t care about the future. I couldn’t see anything but the present, and that was just fine.

Chapter Sixteen

It was a week after we returned from Portland before Mom invited me and Melody over to the Adams' house for dinner. She sent Avery to Jason's for the night. I was bummed watching him leave. My contact with him at that point was nonexistent. I'd been doing nothing besides teaching VBS and hanging out with Dad, which was great, but come on, Avery and I had a lot of relationship mending to do.

Mom made spaghetti and meatballs for dinner. The three of us sat around the unfamiliar dining room table slurping up saucy noodles in awkward silence.

Finally, Mom put her fork down and took a long drink of water. "So, I don't know if your dad has said anything to you girls, but we're sort of separated and have been since you left for Portland." She took a deep breath in and then exhaled slowly. "Also, I'm going to have Mike's baby. I'm pregnant."

Melody glared at me. "Damn it! Could you please get your visions tuned into the right frequency or whatever? I'm getting really sick of these crappy surprises!" She stormed down the hall, but then it dawned on her that she wasn't at our house and couldn't escape into our room. She stood in the hallway seething for a moment before running out the front door, slamming it behind her.

I got up to follow her, but Mom put her hand on my forearm. "Let her go. She's going to the park to blow off steam."

I sat back down, defeated. "You've seen this already?" She was so much better at glimpsing than I was. Mom nodded her head.

"Well, what's my reaction?" I huffed.

"You're mad. You knew about the baby already and are wondering why I waited so long to tell Melody. You think I'm a hypocrite for keeping you away from Avery while I was sneaking around with Mike, which I wasn't, by the way. It was a one time thing the day he died."

I so did not need to know the deets. "Okay, but are you going to patch things up with Dad? Or what? Get a divorce?" I tore little pieces from my napkin, arranging them into a neat pile.

"I'm...we're not sure yet. I can't apologize more than I already have to him. He really did not deserve this, but I've got to think of this baby and try to be happy. Do you understand?" Mom laid her hand on mine, quieting the napkin shredding.

"Are you happy?" I blurted out. "With everything else that's going on with Melody and me? I don't think we deserved this either!" I wanted to run and scream and kick something! I didn't. I stayed in my chair.

"Zel, take how you feel about Avery and multiply it by a hundred. Imagine if the separation you two went through this past month lasted for years. Followed by more years of polite hellos and church functions and then he was gone. Wouldn't you do anything to have him back? In any way possible?"

She wiped tears from her cheek with the back of her hand. "I can talk to Mike and see him and laugh with him whenever I want. I know I'm hurting all of you. Despite that, I am happy. Don't get me wrong. I wasn't miserable with your dad. He is a good man, a good father to you girls. But I've been on autopilot for twenty years and I'm done."

Now I could leave. "I'm gonna go find Melody." I stood up, leaned over and hugged her. "I'm glad you finally said something. I won't shut you out. I just need time."

Mom hugged me tight. "That's fair." She brushed my hair back from my forehead. "I love you Hazel Grace."

That night Melody and I lay in our beds not sleeping, not talking, just staring at the ceiling.

After we'd come home from dinner with Mom, I'd told Dad that we knew about the baby. He'd looked devastated. "I'm going to turn in for the night," was all he'd said and then went into his bedroom and shut the door.

There was a light tapping on the window. We both sat up in bed to see what it was.

Avery waved and then motioned for me to come outside. I checked with Melody.

"Do whatever you want. I guess the Adams men are too irresistible to the redheads in this family." Melody rolled over, turning her back to me. She was reminding me more and more of Aunt Hazel every day. She was going to be an excellent Lookout.

As quietly as I could, I yanked on a pair of shorts underneath my beloved Minnie Mouse nightshirt. Since Dad had removed the desk from our room while we were in Portland to discourage the exact kind of behavior I was about to display, I took out the stepstool I'd stashed under my bed. Barefoot, I climbed up it and slid effortlessly out the window.

Avery grabbed me, pinning me against the side of the house and whispered in my ear, "Are you opposed to rushing back into things?"

"No, rushing's good," I said, nearly breathless.

He kissed me. Finally. A good, long, electricity sparking, sirens blaring, lip numbing sort of kiss. But that wasn't what let me know that all was forgiven between us.

"You know that nightshirt makes me totally hot," he said.

That was.

I giggled and pushed him off of me. "C'mon, let's get away from the house."

We walked hand in hand to the park across the street. Avery's truck was in the parking lot. "We can go sit in the truck if you want," he laughed, "it's a little more private than the park bench."

I took his arm and put it around my shoulders. "Pervert."

He brought me to him, kissing the top of my head. "Whatever. You love me."

"I do love you. How is it that you love me though? I thought you were going to hate me forever and then you were so quick to forgive." We got in the truck.

Avery put his hand on my inner thigh and pulled me closer. His touch sent a shockwave right through me. How I had missed him! He let his hand rest on my knee. "I talked to Claire every day. I know that's more than you knew went on...we weren't trying to be sneaky, we both just didn't want to do any more harm to you than I'd already done."

I nodded. "I'm glad you were careful, I was really messed up."

He squeezed my knee. "From the day after you met your grandma until the day you came home, she told me everything your grandma told you. What she was teaching you to do. How you weren't responsible for my dad's death." He squeezed my knee again. "She told me what happens in the vision you have of me and that you have it *every* night. That's pretty intense, Zel."

I cringed, thinking about my gigantic pregnant belly. The Adams men really were an addiction. "Which part is intense?" Did Claire have to share everything?

He laughed. "All of it. The wreck, the blood, we're old...you're pregnant!"

"About that--"

Avery put his hand up to stop me talking. "Yeah, I can see where you're going with this. Don't freak. I know I'm your trigger, that we have a strong physical connection." He cleared his throat. "Claire seemed really interested in that part."

"God!" I huffed, "I wish she'd get her own strong physical connection and leave mine alone!"

"Really?" Avery laughed again. "'Cause I'm pretty sure that Jason would help her out with that."

"Seriously?"

Avery shrugged.

I took his hand from my knee, intertwining our fingers. "Is it okay if I'm not ready to...you know? I mean, I'm kind of ready, but not ready, ready."

He gazed into my eyes. "I'm not ready, ready either." He put my hand on his heart, right over the spot I'd pulled the bullet from. "I love you, Zellie Wells. We may have an expiration date, but we've got time."

I rewound the last bit, just to hear it again.

The End

Acknowledgements

I would like to thank my Lookout, cover artist, and little sister, Valerie Wallace for inspiring me to write the Zellie books. Thanks also to Sarah Scott, my BFF and the only person on this planet who has read Glimpse as many times as I have.

Kisses to Rob, Gus, and Arlo. I'll always do the welcome home dance for you.

Stacey Wallace Benefiel lives in an orange house in Beaverton, OR with her husband and their two young children. Glimpse is her debut novel.

For more information about Stacey and her books: www.staceywallacebenefiel.com